Without
a stitch

Without a stitch

by Jens Bjørneboe

Translated from the Norwegian
by Walter Barthold

GROVE PRESS, INC. NEW YORK

Without
a stitch

I

"You'll be doing it like an angel before you turn nineteen," said Dr. Peterson as he leaned over me.

I was lying on my stomach before him, with no panties on and with nothing but a little shirt over my shoulders. I spread my legs and raised my hips to give him room to reach up under my stomach from behind in his usual way. I lay waiting, then felt the warmth of his hand against my thighs. I felt it slide down and then up along my front. Dr. Peterson closed his palm over my flower. I put my face down and shut my eyes. He placed his other hand on the little triangle at the base of my spine and massaged carefully, while everything below my waist turned warm and loose. Then one of his fingers slipped slowly down the groove between my buttocks, and I got that wonderful feeling that comes nowhere else.

Dr. Peterson is a specialist in the orgasm. He knows his field from top to bottom, being both gynecologist and psychiatrist and specializing in frigid women. No one knows how many women, young ones especially, Dr. Peterson has helped to achieve real pleasure from love. Only his files (which he keeps for the treatise he is working on) know who his patients have been. I am really not exaggerating when I say that my life began on the day I knocked on his office door—after-hours and without seeing his receptionist. I haven't the slightest doubt that he will go far in the world of science and that he will be numbered among woman-kind's great benefactors.

Let me start from the beginning, first with a word about myself. No, first I must express the gratitude I feel toward him. He has made a woman out of me and taught me what an inexhaustible source of vitality we all have in our own bodies and senses, if only they are treated right. I mean what I say by "treated," too. Also, it was Brita who gave me Dr. Peterson's name and address, so I should thank her as well. The most remarkable thing of all is that the whole change happened after only a few weeks' treatment by Dr. Peterson, each time after office hours and at almost no charge. He used to say that he needed patients like me to build up the store of statistical material for the research he was carrying on.

I was about eighteen and a half the first time I stood outside his door, clutching the slip of paper Brita had given me with his name and address on it. I was nervous and self-conscious as I waited to see if he would answer the door. I found myself almost hoping he had forgotten my appointment.

I look rather thin and delicate with my clothes on. I'm so blonde my hair is almost white, and I cut it quite short, giving myself a boyish look. (This has a strongly erotic effect on some men.) But with my clothes off, no one is apt to take me for a boy. Thin as I am, I have an unusually round and supple bottom. I'm broad in the hips and have a fairly large bust that seems almost to point upward. Actually my breasts turn outward a bit and have fine rosy nipples that come to a nice head. By rubbing them a little, I can make them grow big and stiff in no time. I can take them in my mouth and lick them or suck on them—a trick I learned when I was around the age of fifteen or sixteen and liked so much I've kept it up ever since. That may be one reason why my breasts have grown so firm and developed so well. I don't know. Of course I learned a lot of other things I could do with myself, whether I was alone in the bathroom or lying in bed at night. But that was a good deal earlier, I think when I was about twelve or thirteen.

Brita and I were classmates, but for a long time we couldn't stand each other. Now I know why I didn't like her: for one thing, she was disgustingly attractive to boys, and then she was really splendid to look at under the shower after gym class. A bit stronger and more rounded than I, she was thin as a rail at the waist, with a perfectly straight back that seemed to grow like a tree trunk from her hips. We used to splash cold water at each other whenever we had the chance. In a way, I both liked and detested her.

We first became real friends about a year before she sent me to see Dr. Peterson. With that she did something for me that has meant more to me than anything she had done in the course of that whole year.

Our friendship began with a real fight—in dead earnest, with scratching, hair-pulling, and fists. She was strong and hurt me, but I enjoyed the fight anyway, if only because we came in such close contact with each other.

This all happened on a trip our class was taking together. The teacher had to separate Brita and me and force us to make up. She even made us share a room that night to prove we were friends again. This made both of us so mad that we wept with rage, but the others all laughed at us, so we pretended to make up just to disappoint them. Of course the teacher didn't know what we were fighting about. She thought we had just been teasing each other, but it went deeper than that. I remember when I was little and had to let my mother give me an enema—I both enjoyed it and didn't like it. I had the same kind of feeling about Brita. What was more, she was so damned good at math and science, while I was not good at much besides writing themes. But I was best in the class at that.

In those days I used to talk once in a while with my other girl friends about something that had me worried. I mean about how I could never really make it work when I was with a boy. I never could have an orgasm, and it was really miserable, since many times when I was sleeping with someone I'd get all hot and bothered and be well on the way, but just when it started feeling as if everything below my waist was melting, just as I started floating away and said to myself, "Now! Here it comes," right then something just shut off and stopped the whole business. As soon as I could feel the boy becoming bigger and bigger inside me, tensing his muscles and getting hard as a rock while he groaned or shouted or sobbed, right then I became cold and distant and felt as though everything inside me had come to a standstill. It was enough to make me weep, and as he would pull himself out of me, all wet and soft, feeling like a damp little lump down below, there I was without having had any fun at all out of it.

I was miserable about this, and I turned bitter. I actually got more pleasure out of something quite different—I mean teasing boys as far along as I could, lying down with them and letting them take my panties off, letting them do all they wanted with me for as long as possible, and then, just when they were going out of their minds, suddenly playing virgin with them and saying, "No! I don't want to! Not with you anyway." Just to lie there next to them, making fools of them if I could, touching them, holding them gently by the testicles, running my fingers up to the heads of their penises, but never letting them in me—or best of all, just letting them in half-way for a second, then twisting away with: "No! Put your clothes back on!"

Of course this kind of game wasn't all fun for me either, but anyway it was better than being left without having had anything out of it when the boy always managed to come with a gush and was so contented afterward. It took will power to stop things in time to make sure that he'd have to lie there with unfinished business, just like me.

I talked about all this with the other girls, and it turned out that things were just the same with a lot of them—they didn't have real orgasms either. Knowing that others had the same problem was some consolation, but only a little, and I began to worry that I really was incurably frigid for life or else maybe a lesbian who liked only girls. And I did have to admit that it was fun seeing other girls in the nude, and I enjoyed their touching me. I never talked about any of this with Brita, because I knew that she had read a lot and knew so much, and I was afraid of that malicious, sarcastic sneer of hers when she would raise one eyebrow and at the same time smile with the other corner of her mouth. But I could take care of myself too, and I knew she was a little wary of my sharp tongue.

On this trip that our class took, we spent the night in a folk high school that was vacated between semesters. Brita and I had had this spat, and I was sure I had taken her down a peg. We were both as mad as could be, and I felt the tears coming on. We had been sniping at each other for almost half an hour, and yet I took a certain pleasure in it. Anyway, we had been hurting each other's feelings and making fools of each other when she suddenly leaned forward and said, with almost all the others listening, "We all know what makes you so hysterical, Lillian. You're as frigid as an old-maid schoolteacher!"

I rushed at her and with my first swing hit her one right below the ear. We rolled around on the floor until the teacher heard our screams and the other girls' laughter and came running. They had to pull us apart, and that's when it was decided we should share a room that night. The dormitory had double rooms, each with its own bathroom and shower. Brita and I did what we were told without showing our feelings so the others couldn't laugh at our expense. They all knew not only that our fight was in dead earnest but also that it had been coming on for a long time. After eating supper and sitting by the fireplace with the others for a while, we went quietly up to our room.

As soon as we were alone, we stopped in our tracks and glared at each other. I could feel the tears coming, and I was so angry and humiliated I just had to say something. I couldn't think of anything smart and so ended up with, "You bitch, you! I hate you! I despise you!"

The tears kept on trying to force their way out, but I fought them back.

"You're the most repulsive slut in the whole class," Brita answered. "You're the stupidest, nastiest bitch I know!"

We stood looking at each other, each with eyelashes glistening. We stood erect, arms at our sides, as if the wind had been knocked out of us. We were fighting back the tears and had no strength left for anything else.

Brita sat down on a chair, her dark blond hair hanging over her face. She stared at the floor. "You can use the bathroom first," she said weakly.

I got almost completely undressed while she sat and waited without moving, her face still down. At the bathroom door, I turned and said, "Those dumb sheep down there think we've already become friends."

I shut myself in the shower and began giving myself a thorough bath. It took time, and just as I was soaping myself between the legs, first in front, then in back, the door opened and Brita walked into the small shower room. She had undressed, so we were both stark naked. We were about the same height and stood face to face. I had straightened up and pulled my legs together and was holding the washcloth in my hand. Brita's eyes were damp. She looked awfully sweet, and that scornful sneer of hers was gone.

"But then don't you think we might just as well be friends?" she said, and had to clear her throat. She was standing right up to me, and our breasts, which were at about the same level (mine were a tiny bit lower), came so close together that my right breast brushed against her left nipple. It felt exactly as though a flame had shot through me. My knees grew weak and my spine soft, and a powerful, warm tingling began in my breasts and below my waist. A lump rose in my throat when I saw that she was on the verge of tears again. A few tears of my own squeezed out, and I told her, "Yes." With that lump in my throat, it was all I could do to whisper it.

When she heard my answer, she put her arms around my neck. I dropped the washcloth to the floor and put my arms around her shoulders, letting them slide down to the small of her back and then just far enough so that I felt the white half-moons of her buttocks against the sides of my hands. In front, I could feel her whole body, dry and warm and indescribably soft. Our breasts were pressed together, and we stood there unable to let go of each other, glued together from our cheeks down to our knees. I could taste the salt on her face. We kissed each other on the cheek, then on the corner of the mouth, then squarely on the mouth, just as if she were a boy. She tasted of warmth and flowers, and we embraced until we almost collapsed on the floor. She had pressed her knee between my legs, which suited me fine.

When we let go of each other, I was so dizzy I nearly fell over backward. The front of my body felt on fire, but most of all around my flower. I'd been hoping she would touch me there, but she hadn't.

She just stood motionless. Now she gave a sort of wry smile and said, "So we've become friends after all, Lillian. Shall we go to bed?" She kept on smiling in a gentle, kittenish way.

"You . . . you haven't had your shower yet," was all I could manage to answer.

"I can take it afterward," she said, "and I'm not the least bit dirty anyway. You can come in my bed first."

"May I?" I said and swallowed hard. She smiled again.

"Yes," she whispered. So we walked hand in hand into the bedroom. It was quite light there, because it was summer and still twilight outside. Her bed was ready with the spread removed and the covers turned down. It occurred to me that I should put my pajamas on first, but I didn't feel like it. All I wanted was to get under the covers with her and feel her soft body again.

I lay down and pulled the covers halfway over me. She sat for a moment on the edge of the bed. "Lillian," she said.

"Yes?"

"That was nasty of me to say what I said."

"What are you talking about?" I said and put my hand on her lap. I'd been thinking all along about how I could get to touch her there as if by accident, but all I could manage at first was to put my hand half on her lap and half against her stomach. I felt the darkish, silky hair of her flower touch my fingers.

"I said you were frigid," she went on. "That was nasty, and I didn't mean it. Will you forgive me?"

"Maybe it's true," I said and pressed the palm of

my hand against her stomach. "I don't ever really come with boys."

I waited impatiently for her to get in bed with me, but she didn't move. She looked at my face and suddenly ran her fingers through my hair, scratching my scalp gently, as if she enjoyed keeping her hand there, or as if the hand were a little animal that kept warm in my hair and liked to play in it.

"It doesn't mean a thing that you can't manage it with boys," she said. "An awful lot of us have the same trouble at our age. Can you only come when you're alone? When you lie there and do it by yourself?"

"When I do that, it works," I said softly. I was enjoying the conversation, but hoping we could soon continue it under the covers. Her breasts seemed so big and white in the dusk, and they looked soft, though their shape was firm enough.

"So when you do it by yourself, you get a real orgasm?"

"Yes," I said frankly, "but I'd much rather do it with someone else, if I could just manage it. But don't sit there and shiver. You'll catch cold."

My hand crept up, and I couldn't let her breasts alone. I touched one of them gently, from underneath.

All at once she bent over and lay her head on my chest. Slowly she pushed her face against my left breast and breathed warmly against it several times, pushing warm air along her cheek. Then she began to lick carefully around my nipple in little circles. With her lips closed, she rubbed her mouth over the tip of the nipple, then took it gently in her mouth and flicked her tongue against it with small, quick move-

ments. She was only halfway on the bed. I could feel
my nipple swell. She bit it gently, then started sucking hard on the whole nipple and a good part of the
breast with it. Her mouth felt warm and nice to be in.
I tingled over my whole body, and I shut my eyes and
pulled her in bed. I reached around behind her so that
the fingers of my one hand got into the groove between her buttocks.

"Ah!" she gasped and lay still, keeping my breast
in her mouth but not sucking on it.

"Are you sensitive there?" I asked and let my
fingers slide back and forth along the groove, up to
the base of her spine and then down toward her
flower. As my index finger went by the small, tight
opening about halfway down, I felt her jerk slightly,
and I let my finger rub gently right over the closed,
firm little hole itself and then in circles around it.
Then around the bottom of the groove. Brita had
grown quite still. She lay holding me tight, almost
stiff, except when my fingers touched that one place.
Then a sudden jerk would go through her.

"Are you sensitive there?" I asked again.

Her voice was thick and unclear. "Oh Jesus!" she
said. "My God, I'm dying."

But she remained quite still. Then I noticed that
she was arching her back so that her hips moved up
and it was easier for me to get my fingers into the
groove. For a moment I was afraid she would pass
out, but I was getting so much pleasure out of being
with her that I couldn't interrupt things. What's more,
I felt her pleasure as if it were my own—it made me
proud and happy. She lay quietly, holding me tight.

Down below my waist I felt warm from something

tingling there. It almost hurt, and I reached my free hand down and felt between my legs. I was soaking wet, and because I was lying on my back, the smooth, warm fluid ran back down between my buttocks so that I was damp and slick at every opening. I felt pain right at my flower and down toward my knees, and I hoped she would come to herself and do something with me. I kept one hand between the damp, warm halves of her bottom, and I wanted to use the other to find out what she was like in front, but I was too shy. I just kept massaging her in back and feeling the tight little muscle around the opening. Each time I touched her directly on the soft, closed-up hole itself, she would jerk once again and almost scare me. Otherwise she just clung fiercely to me. The transition came quite suddenly.

All at once she stopped being passive. A couple of violent shudders went through her, and she raised her head and kissed me on the mouth, nearly sucking the tongue out of me. We each flowed into the other's mouth. Finally something like what I had been waiting for happened. She took my hand and pulled it up between her legs. I thought I would faint when I felt the dampness and the soft, silky hair and closed my fingers around the smooth, turned-out part of her sex. She pulled up her knees, so that I almost lost my grip, then tensed herself like a steel spring. At the same time, she kissed me and lay down on me so our breasts pressed against each other. It sounded as if she was crying.

I had one hand behind her and one in front, and I was trying to rub both places at the same time. Then she started to come—her whole body tensed up all it could, then began to relax. I myself was damp, warm, and unsatisfied. She lay still for a couple of seconds, and I was glad to feel the palm of her hand on the inside of my leg, just above the knee. Then it moved upward.

Her fingers traveled back and forth between my legs, up where the skin is thin and sensitive. I felt her hand move in where I was wet and slick—at first in back, between my buttocks, and then up along the midline between my legs. I could have screamed when I felt her hand brush over that fuzzy, soft little creature of mine—on the right place. Outside, in my hair, I was moist from sweat, but inside I was wet from something quite different. She put one finger in and searched for that little growth that seems to pull together every nerve in my body. She found it and at that moment kissed me on the mouth so that we melted together completely. Her fingers caressed me gently on the clitoris, and I let go of her in back but kept my arm around her. Then I let go of her altogether and just lay like an old rag. Right then it happened, what had never happened before: I reached a climax with someone else and not by myself. A stream of molten metal ran through my body, and I flung my legs around her, weeping out loud.

We remained like that for some time, damp and warm, with our arms around each other's neck. Her long hair covered my face. At length she said, "It's just as well Miss Moe doesn't know what a good idea she had. If she could only see what good friends we've become, it would kill her."

She raised her head and looked at me with that old, sarcastic smile of hers. But there was no evil in it now. We just laughed. She was cheerful, sweet, and affectionate.

We shared a chocolate bar afterward, then went to the bathroom together, since she still hadn't taken her shower. We were rested by now, and it was lovely to stand together under the shower. I can remember to this day the taste of her nipples and the warm, fresh water. As I licked and sucked at her breasts, the nipples got big again, and I started getting hot myself. I washed her in back, then carefully in front. We dried each other thoroughly and lay down in my bed.

Next morning we showered together again. For the rest of that school year we were the best of friends and never cared about anyone else in the class.

What used to bother me in those days was a guilty conscience over what we had done, plus the thought of what parents, relatives, and teachers would have said if they had known what good times we had together. You'd think we'd harmed someone by doing something that gave us both pleasure and caused pain to no one. When I would sit doing my homework or writing a theme, and just lifted my hand toward my face in thought, I would often notice that lovely, fresh fragrance of her flower, and the faint, marvelous scent of her freshly washed backside—which was almost better still. But I had, as I say, a guilty conscience nevertheless, in spite of the fact that no one knew about it and it did no one any harm.

But it didn't bother me enough to keep Brita and me from having fun together at every opportunity. It wasn't too often anyway, because we had to be careful about all the others. We avoided going to the toilet together, which girls often do otherwise, and we never embraced when others were looking. Occasionally it would be a long time before we had the chance to be really happy together. But a change was taking place in me: I seemed to be coming back to life again, and I was much happier than before, even with that troublesome conscience of mine and in spite of how I often thought about boys and about how it would be if I tried it with a boy again. It began to frighten me, but every time I talked to a boy I couldn't help thinking of how he must look with his trousers off. I was dying to have a look at that wonderful, changeable organ again—stiff and hard, long and moist, or else small, soft and flabby, slick and supple.

It wasn't too long before I had the chance to try myself out on a boy again. His name was Henry.

Henry was awfully sweet, and just a couple of years older than me. He had curly blond hair and wasn't especially tall or husky—you could almost call him the delicate type. He was a bit bashful and rather inexperienced, and I had seen him now and then at school parties and dances.

It was summer, about a month after the school trip on which Brita and I became friends. Henry and I had been to a party at a girl's house, and I'd been wanting him all evening. I held hands with him, and we gave each other little kisses while we danced, so it was only natural for us to leave for home together. Since Henry's parents were away on a trip, we went to his house when the party was over.

Henry began by finding something to drink in his father's cabinet and then turned the record-player on —a pretty dull way to start things off, I thought.

When he got around to seducing me, it became down-right comical, but I shut my eyes and managed to keep a straight face. He finally got up nerve enough to put one finger inside the edge of my panties. By this time I was good and hot and felt like getting things going in a proper way, but at the same time I was a little shy. Henry sneaked his whole hand under the edge of my panties and found his way to my flower, where he began rubbing his fingers against my hair. He took long enough about it, too. Next he ventured to the opening itself and got his finger wet. Then he put his finger in all the way, but he did it wrong—just stuck it in and pulled it out again. He didn't even look for that dangerous beautiful spot that holds all my feelings, and I couldn't help thinking of Brita's skillful, alert fingers. *There* was someone who knew something about the female body. You couldn't say that about Henry, sweet as he was. He hadn't taken off my bra or really done anything at all to warm me up, like rubbing the small of my back. To make a long story short, things didn't look too prom-ising.

I sat up straight on the sofa, grabbed the highball glass, and emptied it in one long pull. I felt the effect right away, and that got me over my shyness. He was going at it in the same way with his finger, though it was hard for him to get at me when I leaned forward. Then I dropped my hand in his lap, accidentally of course, and felt around with the back of it. There was no doubt that he was in fighting trim now, and a shudder went through him when he felt my hand. So I gave him a long, deep kiss on the lips. I stuck my tongue into his mouth and noticed that he stopped moving his hand. It was unbelievable how inexperienced Henry was, and in a way that only got me all the more excited. I was almost more hot and bothered there with him than when I was with Brita.

I reached underneath his belt, felt my way through his shirt and underpants and took hold of that stiff creature of his. Henry lowered his head and groaned from shock. You could tell this was the first time he'd ever known a girl to take the initiative. I really thought he was going to pass out. I just held my hand around the thickest part of his sex and played gently with it. Then I let my hand slip farther in, all the way to the root of the thing and his hair. The effect of all this was obvious from the way Henry was panting. I took him carefully around the stones, and now I found exactly what I wanted to know— he was not one of those huge, king-sized fellows, but about average in size, and his testicles were small and quite hard. That's the way I liked it.

Henry was almost in convulsions. I touched him out at the tip of his pecker with one finger and felt that it was wet with that lovely secretion that's smoother than anything else in the world. But there was skin covering the whole head of the creature itself.

"Henry?" I said.

"Yes," he groaned softly.

"You're just my size," I continued. "Which is your room around here?"

I pulled my hand away quickly and got up. He sat there on the sofa like a limp rag, then got up and swallowed. He looked weak.

"This way," he said and walked toward the hall.

I followed him the few steps through the hall and there we were, face to face in the room that had been his as a boy. I felt that I had to say something to him but first I kicked off my shoes and pulled down my skirt and panties. I was naked from the waist down.

"You mustn't think I'm really this kind of girl," I said.

Henry just swallowed and began to fumble with his shoelaces. That took a while, and by the time he had his shoes and socks off I didn't have a stitch left on me. The way he fooled with his tie and shirt was enough to make you weep. I went over to him and did what I'd been wanting to all along. Under his thin underdrawers, his lovely organ stood right out, bent upward toward his stomach. The head was covered with skin, so only a bit of the red tip was visible. That part actually shone. His scrotum looked nice and brown, with not too much hair on it, and the stones quite visible. I took hold of them.

Henry flung his shirt on the floor and grabbed me by the waist. I let go of his scrotum and pulled myself away. I wanted to see him all naked first. "Take your undershirt off," I said.

He pulled it over his head and was naked. He made an attractive sight. Henry *was* a sweet boy, I decided. That frail, boyish body almost disappeared alongside that little thing that pointed slightly upward and now looked enormous. I walked over to him and placed myself where it would just touch my stomach. At this point he could hardly stand up any more. He grabbed me by the shoulders and pulled me over to the bed. I would have liked to look at him longer, but I flung myself down on the sheets, jerking the pillow out of the way so I was flat on my back. He lay down beside me and then flung himself right on top of me. It was way too soon, but I spread my legs and gave him a chance. He fumbled around a bit and couldn't find his way at all, so I put my right hand around his org̱ . and guided the head of it into the opening of my flower.

The size of it was just right, and I thought I'd about die when he put it in the first inch or so. It was just right—hurt a tiny bit and felt heavenly. I felt it throughout my body, from my neck all the way to the tendons in back of my knees. I could feel every sixteenth of an inch as he came farther in. He went all the way in and then came out again.

All at once I could tell that I wasn't going to make it. Everything was wrong. He kept at it, in and out, in and out, and now it hurt because the feelings there had stopped. I lay with my legs apart and all my secrets out in the open, and there wasn't the least bit of fun to it. I felt him get hard as iron inside me, and at the same time my mother's and grandmother's faces appeared before me. God Almighty, what would they have said if they could have seen this? I hadn't taken any precautions either, so what if something went wrong to boot? I grew stiff and cold and felt ashamed that I had reached under his trousers. I felt ashamed of everything and knew I had a guilty conscience. I was about to twist away from him, so at least I'd have the pleasure of keeping him from having any fun out of it, but it was too late. He came suddenly, clinging to me and burying his face next to my shoulder, and at the same time pulled his organ much too quickly out of me and up, so that all of his hot, slippery liquid shot out on my stomach. It gushed from him several times, with me lying there, wet and unsatisfied. He flung himself over on his side, happy and contented.

I was really in an awful mood. In order to get something out of all the feelings that had been aroused in me and then disappointed, but still not all gone, I took his little wet thing between my fingers and felt how slippery it was. Just holding it gave me some consolation anyway.

I was furious, and I detested Henry.

When I'd been holding it for a minute or so, I noticed that it was beginning to get big again. It was still not hard, but it was growing steadily. I took a look at it, and by now it was about half stiff. Henry was ready to start over. I made up my mind to get revenge this time. And I did a good job of it. First I played with him until he was just as big and hard as the first time. The skin still didn't slide back from the head. That's just the way he was. I tickled him gently around the testicles and could see the effect. I put his hand in between my legs, but he couldn't do it properly with me lying as I was. That didn't make a bit of difference, because this time I had something else in mind. He didn't touch my breasts or do anything else—all he wanted was to get back in. I made him wait for almost ten minutes, till he begged, pleaded, and almost cried. I told him I didn't want to. It hadn't (and this was the truth) done me any good to have him in me. But he kept on begging, while I pressed my legs together and gave in just a bit at a time.

"All right," I said. "I'll do it for your sake."

So I spread my legs and let him in. Now I was wide awake and counting the seconds. It would take him longer this time, but I was cold as ice and not feeling a thing. He got going at full speed, just like the last time, and I waited to feel that first tensing of his muscles as he'd seem to get still bigger inside me. Time went by, and then I could tell it was beginning. Suddenly I twisted over on my side and got him out of me. At first he didn't understand and tried to start up again—got on top of me and tried to get in. I took him gently by his pecker and said, "No! I don't want to."

He pleaded with me until tears came to his eyes, and now it was me who was having the fun. This time mother and grandmother were on *my* side. I wasn't doing anything wrong.

Henry had lost his self-control. He tried to use force, but only made a fool of himself. He went back to begging and asked if I'd please let him go on.

Finally I said yes, straightened out and opened my legs. He almost screamed at the chance, and his organ slipped right into me; it fit fine, but didn't do me a bit of good. I let him get going again, and when he began to take firmer hold of me and tense himself inside me, I quickly pulled my legs together and pushed him out.

I let him start up two more times, then put on my bra and blouse and stood in front of him, naked below the waist. He was pale and stooped over, and I knew he'd suffered as much as I had. He looked at me as though he could kill me, but Henry was a nice, well-behaved boy and didn't do a thing. I slowly put my skirt and panties back on and went out in the hall, where my light summer coat was hanging. Henry took me home and asked if he could see me again. I let him take me out all summer and well into the fall, and I always treated him the same way. Mother and grandmother could be proud of me! The remarkable thing was that he put up with this treatment and got to be quite dependent on me even though I allowed him less and less, sometimes nothing at all or just putting the tip in for no more than a second. Henry stayed in love with me through it all.

What strange creatures humans are.

After this unsuccessful experiment with Henry, it was even better to go back to Brita. Something was keeping me from having an orgasm with men. Something or other inside me just came to a standstill, since I knew I didn't lack the desire.

When Brita and I had our occasional chances to be alone and undisturbed, we had many strange experiences. But she was always the one who had to begin, because I was bashful until the tingling in my flower became so powerful that I went ahead and did what I felt like with her. Once we had really gotten underway, I was often the more ardent.

One of the first times we were alone at my house, Brita was spending the night there. My father used to be away a lot, but my mother was usually at home evenings. We have a house and garden a little way from town. My parents were going to a party together, my brother was away on a trip, and after eight o'clock Brita and I were alone. Both of us were thinking of the same thing from the start. Brita gave me that

friendly, ironic smile of hers, but even she was a little hesitant.

In the cupboard was a bottle of gin and some bottles of wine. We each had a couple of good-sized drinks. Brita's smile got more mischievous, she began looking slier, and while we were sitting on the sofa she lay down with her head in my lap. She took one of my fingers and chewed gently on it. Then she licked where the skin is thin between my fingers and afterward on the inside of my wrists. She's not so dumb when it comes to anatomy. The minute she touched me, I got lightheaded and a little dizzy, and something started running in the small of my back. She got up and placed me so that my head was in her lap. I could feel her warm mouth and breath against my ear. She licked carefully at the inside of my ear, then suddenly pushed her tongue all the way in. It ran through my whole body, and I felt myself shudder. I had never known how sensitive my ears were. She rubbed my neck, then all at once leaned back. She was wearing slacks and a light summer shirt, and now she took the shirt off, while I kept my head in her lap. She leaned forward and turned my face up.

"Open your mouth," she said.

Her left breast was hanging soft and round right over my face, and when I opened my mouth I knew what was going to happen. She leaned forward until her firm little nipple came in between my lips. I held it without doing anything, and looked into those gray eyes surrounded by the big lashes. She smiled with her mouth closed, as if it hurt somewhere. Gradually I began to move my tongue against the tidbit between my lips. Every movement was reflected in

Brita's face, around her mouth and in her eyes. I sucked harder and felt the smooth little lump get stiffer and stiffer in my mouth. When it had sprung forth in full bloom, Brita pulled it from my lips and swung her shoulders so that I got her other breast to work on—it grew big right away from the massaging I gave it with my tongue. Then Brita put her hand under my shirt (I was dressed just like her, except for blue jeans instead of slacks) and took hold of the tip of one of my breasts. A shudder passed through me as she turned the nipple back and forth between her fingers. She straightened up and sat over me with her two wet, swollen nipples. It was a lovely sight to look up at.

Then she pulled my shirt out of my blue jeans and took off my bra. We stayed like that for a while, with our tight pants on and naked above the waist. She lay back on the sofa, and I slid along after her until we faced each other. We lay there, each with her buttered side against the other, and rubbed our breasts together. I noticed once more that hers were wet and mine were dry.

I got up and took her by the hand. She came along willingly, and with full glasses in our hands we walked up the stairs to the second floor.

"Shall we use the bathroom or the bedroom?" I asked.

"The bathroom . . . first," said Brita in a pleased voice. Her eyes were aglow and her cheeks warm and flushed. We walked into the bathroom together.

"I'll wash you," she said and picked out a bar of fragrant English soap from the medicine cabinet.

Suddenly she laughed aloud and held something up. It was my mother's thermometer.

I knew right away what she was thinking about, and I hoped she would do it. She picked up a jar of vaseline and came toward me with the strange little ironic smile that I knew so well.

"Hold onto the bathtub," she said, and I leaned forward and took hold of the edge, still standing up with my jeans on. I could feel the tingling in the small of my back as I waited.

She unfastened the zipper on my blue jeans and pulled them down to my knees. Then she pulled down my panties too. After a moment I felt her pulling my buttocks apart and suddenly a shock went through my body—she had smeared vaseline on one of her fingers and put the finger right on the heart of the matter. She didn't put the finger in, just rubbed vaseline carefully over the opening and around it.

"There!" she said, and I could tell from her voice that she was smiling. "Now you've got to be a good girl, because it's going to hurt a little."

I waited a moment. I felt the cold, hard glass point being pushed into me the first little bit. It was pulled back out and then, quite carefully, put farther in. And it didn't hurt a bit, I'll tell you, but titillated in the loveliest way imaginable. It reminded me of what used to happen when I was a child, the difference being that now, because it was Brita doing it, it was so beautiful I could feel it in every nerve in my body. She moved the point back and forth—I think she was rolling it between her fingers.

"Can't you open your legs more?" she asked.

"No," I said. "Not with my jeans and panties around my knees. But try now." Even while she was talking. I had instinctively leaned far over the side of the tub and arched my back so as to raise my backside as high up as I could.

"Is it better this way?" I asked.

"I can see better now," said Brita and turned the end of the little thing around inside me. "But we'd better go into bed for a while."

It almost hurt when she pulled the thermometer out. I got my jeans off and we dashed into my room where the bed was all made. I lay down on my side, with my back toward her. She leaned over me, and again I felt her finger with the vaseline moving between my buttocks. She smeared on a bit more and pushed the thermometer in again, then turned me over on my stomach and sat down on the edge of the bed. She toyed with me for quite a while, and perhaps the nicest part of the whole thing, since I had grown used to the novel sensation of having something stuck into such a private place, was the feeling of not being embarrassed about it but having complete confidence in Brita, knowing that she wouldn't laugh at me for enjoying it and that I could be completely natural about it and not have to hide anything I felt. I groaned and shuddered every once in a while, mumbling words that neither she nor I understood.

This ecstasy continued until she suddenly jerked the point out. "Ninety-eight point six," she said coldly and calmly. "Just right."

I wanted to tell her that I felt like doing the same thing to her, but I suddenly got embarrassed and couldn't say it. Brita smiled and kissed me on the mouth, putting her tongue deep into me. I began to fool with her slacks, and she reached down, loosened them at the waist, and stood up.

You just wouldn't believe how lovely she looked, standing there naked down to where her thighs began. I pulled her slacks all the way down, then got up and from behind pulled down her panties too. The elastic on them left a narrow red stripe around her slender waist, and I put my hands there and pushed her over to the bed, where she lay down. I took her slacks and panties the rest of the way off, so her feet were free.

Reaching up carefully between her legs, I felt how wet she was in her flower and between the upper part of her thighs. She turned over on her stomach and lay with her face in the pillow. Her back was delightful, rather flat across the shoulders, and she was unbelievably slender at the waist, with hips and buttocks that would remind you of a large fruit, a sort of giant pear all white and lovely with a clean skin, and then with that marvelous split beginning a little below the small of her back. It got so I could hardly stand to look at it, and I suddenly bent down and kissed her right where the two halves begin to divide. She squirmed like a trout on the hook.

I sat on the bed beside her and shook down the thermometer, then picked up the jar of vaseline and put a little on the tip of my right index finger. With my left hand I pulled apart her white buttocks, leaned forward, and looked into the groove. That was absolutely the first time in my whole life I had ever looked at that part of anyone's body, and it was astonishing to see how nice it was. On Brita, anyway, it was exquisite. At the bottom of the groove the color was almost pink, or maybe faintly brownish, while farther out the skin had a yellow tint that faded into white. The opening itself was tiny, without a wrinkle, just tight and lovely. Right there was where I put my index finger with the vaseline, rubbing it in, in tiny circles. Brita shuddered under my hand.

"Oh God," she said and burrowed her face in the pillow.

I picked up the thermometer, dipped the point in the vaseline, and put it against her opening while I held her buttocks as far apart as I could. She shuddered violently the minute she felt it.

"All right now," I said strictly, "you lie still!"

She twisted to and fro, but I kept the point on the outer edge without putting it in. She couldn't bear to wait, so she lifted up her backside and tried in vain to work it in that way. I pushed her down again, spread her buttocks, and then felt sorry for her. The shiny point disappeared, first for about an eighth of an inch into the little hole, which stretched open without resisting. I held it there.

It was strange to watch Brita's struggling back. She said something incomprehensible and then called out, "More, Lillian! Farther in!"

I did as she said and then began to play with the thermometer. I let go of it and let it stand up by itself, then I pulled it out and pushed it back in several times, turned it in my fingers, and stirred it around a little as though in a pan. She gave out with a rather loud groan.

I released the grip I had on her backside with my left hand, and her buttocks closed around the glass tube, so that only the very end stuck out behind. It was nice to look at, and again I turned it about with my right hand, reaching under her stomach with my left to feel the little creature she had up front, where she was now dripping wet.

It was easy to find my way to that groove too, and when I had found her clitoris and had my index finger on it, I did both things at the same time, front and back. I enjoyed it because the effect on her was so powerful. She almost screamed. But it got terribly difficult when she began to thrash about. She flung herself here and there, plunging her hips up and down.

I kept at it anyway, because Brita was enjoying it, and I wanted to do everything to make her glad to be with me. I pushed the thermometer way in and turned it around with a lot more than just the point in her firm little opening, and up front I kept on exciting her clitoris between my index finger and thumb. Brita grew even more violent, and when she turned her face toward me with her eyes closed, I noticed tears forcing their way out between the long lashes. Her whole face was damp. Suddenly she tensed her body and gave a long sob. I could tell she was coming with full force.

A moment later she was quite still.

"Now it's your turn," she said, raising her head and smiling at me.

She meant what she said.

It really was my turn, and I lay down on my stomach with my backside up in the air. She hesitated.

"Hurry!" I said.

"Lift up in back," she said, and I did. Then the thermometer slipped in, once again smooth and cool— but not where it had gone before. I got it in front, and

I screamed, half from fright and half from pleasure. I'd never had a thermometer in there before, and it was marvelous—cold, hard, and just lovely. When she put it in behind I almost jumped up, it was so unexpected.

"Lie on your side," she said.

I did so, sliding my upper leg forward. Now she could switch openings so quickly that I thought it was in both places at the same time. Then she changed over to giving me the same treatment I had given her—front and back at the same time. And I must admit that it worked the way it was supposed to. I'm sure I squirmed and twisted just as much as she had. Everything dissolved, and I could feel myself coming in her quick, skillful hands.

Afterward we took a shower and ate some supper. We had a couple more drinks from my father's cupboard and went to bed together—in the more customary way, that is.

Brita and I kept on getting together two or three times a month all winter long, but at the same time, I was going out every so often with Henry. It was a good thing he was so much in love with me, because he put up with everything it occurred to me to do to him. In any event, he was the cause of my breaking up with both him and Brita. I got scared of him. But that didn't happen until spring.

Of course Henry and I had our troubles finding places to be alone, because my parents watched us much more closely than they did Brita and me. But once in a while we had a chance.

Being with Henry and doing things with him usually

embarrassed me a lot and gave me a guilty conscience, and since I knew that he couldn't make me come I was always thinking up new things to drive him half out of his mind. Whenever I was going to meet him, I took my bra off beforehand, because he always noticed it right away, which gave me the upper hand from the start.

Quite often the things that I did were entirely harmless, and mother and grandmother would not have had the slightest reason to be ashamed of me— but that's because they would not have understood what was actually going on. They would only have seen that I was a good, chaste girl who didn't let Henry do anything improper to me. At such times I was totally moral, sometimes so proper that I wouldn't even let him kiss me. He'd get awfully unhappy on such days, I suppose because he thought I was about to stop seeing him for good.

But I do remember once when we went to the movies together, and I did something altogether indecent with him. On the way there, we'd begun by kissing a little, and he'd put his hand under my sweater and felt my bare breasts.

Inside the theater, I acted totally innocent at first and just held his hand. I knew this was enough to get him steamed up, undoubtedly because I always made sure that he never had an orgasm when he was with me. We sat like that for a while.

But once the lights were out and the picture underway, I put my hand down on his lap and pressed against his crotch. Sure enough, Henry was ready for action, as usual, and I kept on feeling around outside his trousers. Then I opened his fly and put my hand in. I held it there perfectly still for a long time, and Henry began breathing harder and harder. But of course he couldn't make a move because of the people sitting around us.

After a while I felt my way to that fine, rigid pecker of his. It was as stiff as could be, and I had a hard time getting it out through the front of his shorts. I finally managed, and when I had it out I could tell that it was all Henry could do to sit still. But he had to anyway.

I squeezed his organ and heard him gasp. He clenched his fists and lowered his head a bit. I took hold of it at the base and moved out toward the end —it was damp and slippery at the tip. With my two fingers I pulled his foreskin back, the entire, round, sensitive lump at the end stood exposed. His skin there was fairly tight, and I'm sure that what I did hurt him a bit. But he liked it all the more. I held him for some time without moving my fingers, then began to rub my index finger over the little opening at the tip. In the same way, I rubbed around the rim where the head ends and the skin begins. I was beginning to get pretty hot and bothered myself, and I was thinking how lovely it would have been if I could really have enjoyed Henry. (At that time, I had no idea *why* I couldn't.) But I knew that I couldn't, which renewed my determination. I kept on playing with his pecker for almost the whole performance, and it was stiff for about two full hours. Afterward Henry could hardly walk, and he complained of a pain down there.

I played this game a lot when I was with Henry—

fooling around with him in different ways without giving him a chance to touch me. Neither tears nor pleading did him any good.

What used to really get him was when I would take his trousers off, or open them up all the way, and then slowly pull his foreskin back, holding him by the testicles with one hand and putting the fingertips of the other hand around the head of his pecker, almost without moving them.

But it was one particular evening that settled things between Henry and me. We were at his house, as on the first evening we had been together, and his parents were away on a trip, so we had a full evening ahead of us. We had something to drink, which helped overcome my shyness and my guilty conscience. As usual, I had no bra on, and it was early spring—late March or early April. When he went out to the kitchen, I took my panties off too.

He came back, sat down next to me, and started in under my blouse. That he was allowed to do. While he was at it, I lay back and pulled up my skirt so he could see that I had nothing on under there either. He turned white, and I could tell he knew that I was up to something with him. I put my legs up across his lap, holding them so close together he couldn't even get a finger in.

He had his hand on my tummy, with the palm against my hair. I took a sip of my drink and wanted so much just to be nice to him and go to bed. But I knew it would mean lots of fun for him and nothing for me. I felt sure that Henry had made me frigid for good, and if he hadn't already got what was coming to him he was going to tonight. I'd made up my mind to go just as far as would give me pleasure and from then on let him look out for himself.

I got up, pulled my dress over my head, and stood before him naked as the day I was born. Then I lay down at the other end of the sofa and raised my knees toward him so that he could see everything there was to see.

He just looked at it, without making a move.

"Come on," I said. "Come over here and have a good look. But first, you get undressed too."

Trembling, Henry got up and took his clothes off. He came over and stood beside me, his pecker sticking straight out right next to my chest. It actually pointed up quite a bit. I moved my face toward it, put one hand around his testicles, and placed my mouth next to that hot, damp, hard-as-rock creature of his. I breathed on it. Henry was almost in tears.

"Lillian," he said softly, "can't I, please, tonight?"

I had his sex right in front of me, and I felt a strange desire to take it in my mouth. But I didn't dare. Instead I gave it a good, wet kiss at the tip. At that very second it occurred to me what mother would have said about this, which made me furious with Henry. I took his pecker in my hand and pressed it against my breasts. I rubbed it hard against them and then stopped.

"No, Henry," I answered. "It would just ruin everything between us."

I turned over and stretched out on the sofa before him. He lay down too, but all he got was my back. I wondered why he couldn't think up some of the things Brita could, and I felt like telling him what to do, but my feeling of shame returned and I couldn't get a word out. However, my conscience was clear for not having let him do anything. I turned around toward him so that we lay face to face and could kiss each other on the mouth. I really felt much more like kissing him somewhere else. I raised my head and looked down at him, there where he was slippery and nice. I was just crazy about it, and it fit me so well, both in thickness and in length. Henry was breathing with great effort.

I got up.

"Sit down on that chair over there," I said, pointing to a regular dining-room chair. I was furious that the feeling was so strong and that I wanted his organ so much. He went over and sat down on the chair, his pecker sticking up almost along his stomach.

"Sit a little more forward," I went on, "and lean back."

He did, and it made a fine sight.

Then I stood in front of him, and putting my feet far apart, I sat down astride him, just above his knees. His damp, hot thing almost touched my stomach. I moved a little closer, until we sat right up against each other, with nothing but his pecker between us.

"It's better in a different chair," I said, "a softer one."

Henry went over to an armchair, where he sat much farther back, and now the little red tip didn't stick up nearly so far. I sat down on his lap, with my back to him but with my legs together. In that position I could tell I had the damp head about midway between the two openings.

I sat there for a moment, feeling how lovely it

was. Then I slid toward him a bit, and now it was at the right place. It was only my legs being together that kept it from getting in. I spread them apart, and it slipped slowly into me—but not more than an inch. I sat up a little straighter, and it came in about another half inch. For me it was just right, and it struck me again how well his medium-sized sex fitted mine—not too big, not too thick, but just the size that mine could fit like a glove. It was plain heavenly. Now, as we were sitting there without making the slightest move, I felt safe. I had him in me just a lovely little bit. And so long as we didn't move, nothing wrong was happening. I was innocent. I was a virgin.

I shut my eyes and simply felt how good it was to have him that way.

At that moment he leaned farther back and raised his hips up hard. With a shove he was almost all the way in, just about to the bottom. I sprang away from him.

"No!" I said. "You're not supposed to move. Otherwise I won't let you."

I sat down astride him, but the other way around, facing him, with my arms around his neck. I had it in me again, maybe a bit farther than before. I looked at his face. It had changed.

I shifted position slightly, so that I had one knee on each side of him in the roomy armchair, and with his pecker in me just a bit—really only the head. By reaching around under my backside, I could feel all of him that was outside me. It's funny that something made of flesh and blood can get so hard.

"Isn't it good this way?" I said softly. With that, I moved up and down a couple of times, then sat still again. He tossed his head back and forth and twisted his mouth. I moved up and down, ever so slowly, two or three more times. The effect on him was so violent that I began to laugh out loud.

Right away the laughter froze in my throat.

Whatever was wrong with my nice, gentle Henry?

To begin with, he got up without saying a word. He looked as if he was going to kill me. I got really scared of him.

Then he started talking, and I'm not going to repeat what he said. He took me by the wrists, and I noticed how much stronger he was than me. He twisted one arm around behind me, while he said the worst words he could think of. Then he twisted my arm until I was lying over the armrest of the sofa— on my stomach with my backside up in the air, almost like when Brita tried mother's thermometer on me for the first time. But believe you me, what happened now was something quite different. Henry began spanking me on my bottom with all his strength. I was so frightened that I almost didn't dare scream. I just whimpered. I think he hit me twenty or thirty times.

The strange thing was that in a way I even liked this, although it hurt plenty.

Afterward something happened that surprised me still more, but which didn't scare me, because I understood it. He grabbed me full strength by the wrists, in such a way that he could break my arms over my head. Then he forced me down on the sofa so that I lay back but with my feet on the floor. I noticed that his sex had stayed stiff through the whole spanking.

He pressed my wrists down next to my head, and I could feel his pecker finding its way in without help. This time not a bit of it was left outside, and there were no small, careful movements; it was all the way to the bottom and in and out as rough as could be. Not so very many times either, as excited as Henry was. Then he took still firmer hold and pressed down on me with his full weight while he let his whole load gush into my insides.

As soon as he was through, he sprang up and said, "Go to hell!"

He threw a quilt over me and left me lying there. I turned over on my side and noticed that something was all set to happen to me. So I put my hand between my legs and helped things along. It happened, all right, but I was lying under the quilt, and if Henry was looking at me he must have thought my shaking came from crying. I got to go home alone that night, and Henry has never asked me out since.

A couple of days later I told Brita the whole story, everything I had done to Henry and what he had finally done to me.

Brita listened attentively and then became quite serious. It was after this that she told me about Dr. Peterson. She said she was afraid I could get into real trouble and that what Henry had done was understandable and maybe even right.

She said that Dr. Peterson was an orgasm specialist and that he was absolutely the only one who could help me prevent having my relations with men ruined for good.

She made an appointment for me with Dr. Peterson, got him to accept me as a patient, and what's more she put me in "sexual quarantine," as she called it. She refused to play with me until after she heard what Dr. Peterson had to say about it.

Now it came out that it was Dr. Peterson who had helped her achieve orgasms—with boys, too.

This is how I came to be standing in front of Dr. Peterson's office door one fine spring day with Brita's address slip clutched in my sweaty hand.

I was extremely anxious and tense.

I rang three times, and he opened the door. He was a man of quite unusual appearance.

2

"Would you be good enough to get undressed please?" said Dr. Peterson, after he had written down in his book my name, year of birth, previous illnesses, and things like that. He turned his face my way and kept looking at me. Dr. Peterson was dark, with traces of gray in his hair, and about forty years old. His features were well-defined, his face rectangular and narrow at the same time. He wasn't dressed like a doctor, but more like an orderly, in a white coat with no shirt under it.

"Your girl friend told me what your problem was," he said, "and I'm just going to begin with a routine examination. Please take everything off."

He kept looking at me.

I supposed that he had no shirt on under his white coat because it was so warm in the office. I got up and began undressing. Shoes, blouse, slacks, stockings. He kept looking at me. Bra, panties. I felt unusually shy, small, and alone as I stood before him naked, even if he was a doctor.

"Turn around," he said.

I turned my back to him. Dr. Peterson got up from his desk and took off his glasses. He came over and walked around me. He stopped and stared at my breasts and my hips. Once he put the warm palm of his hand on the small of my back. It felt strange. Then he stopped in front of me.

"Stand up straight, please."

I did what he said, and he nodded. Then he smiled.

"Why in the world are you embarrassed?" he asked.

This made me blush, and I couldn't think of an answer. He walked quickly over to his desk and wrote something down.

"Physically you look in excellent shape," he said without looking up. "Your bust and your hips are quite well developed, and on the whole you're very well built. Sit down on the table and cross your legs."

He beckoned me over to one of those funny wheeled tables that have metal supports at one end for women patients to rest their legs in.

I perched on the edge of the table, and he wrote down a few more words. Then he came over to me holding a little hammer with a rubber head.

"You're very well built physically, and you have nothing to be ashamed of. You should be happy and proud to take off your clothes. Have you ever thought about why you're embarrassed?"

"No, uh, yes . . ." I answered. "I don't know. But that's the way it is."

"I'm just going to test your reflexes," he said and tapped gently with the rubber hammer below the knee that was on top. My foot came up like a shot out of a gun. I changed knees, and he repeated the tap—with the same effect.

"All right," he said. "Excellent. Now shut your eyes and put your right index finger on the tip of your nose. Now the left."

I did as he said.

"That's that," said Dr. Peterson. "Now lie down and relax."

I lay down on my back, wondering if I should put my legs in the two supports.

"Shall I . . ." I began.

"Not yet," he said. "Just lie the way you are. But relax. This isn't dangerous. Just be calm, and don't be embarrassed. Every woman has the same things under her clothes as you. Being female is nothing to be ashamed of."

He seemed to be taking it all in his stride, and I felt strongly that I wasn't the first woman who'd undressed in his office. That, of course, was why the room was so warm; Dr. Peterson's office was a place where girls undressed. That's what they came here for. He was standing over me and smiling.

"We can use first names in any event," he went on, "so it will be easier to talk to each other. You must be absolutely frank with me about everything, Lillian, if I'm going to help you, and it's important that you get used to being without clothes in here. You must cure yourself of being shy about anything at all. You are not to be ashamed of anything, and you have nothing to be ashamed of."

He grasped my hand so that our palms were pressed together. With his other hand he rubbed the inner side of my wrist. It had a strange, soothing effect on me. I liked it. His hand slipped up along the inside of my arm. He rubbed me several times from the wrist up to the armpit. I began to hope that he would continue farther up. His fingers were unbelievably alive and light, but strong too when he pressed down a little.

"How is it?" he said. "Do you feel anything?"

"Yes," I said.

Then he put his hand under my armpit with its thin downy hairs. I felt it distinctly, because he had a way of touching me that pierced to the marrow of my bones. I shuddered as he did it. Then he pressed his fingers in my armpit so it tickled. It was lovely, and I felt glad that I was lying naked before him and that he was going to continue the examination. He sat down beside me on the table, keeping his thumb in my armpit.

"Do you like it better being naked now?" he asked.

"Yes," I said and smiled.

"Tell me exactly how it feels," he said. "Exactly."

"It seems to run through my shoulders and down my back."

He nodded.

"Tell me what you'd like me to do," he continued. "But look at me, look me in the eye when you tell me. Is there anything you feel like doing? Don't be ashamed of it. Everyone has certain things he likes to do."

I thought about some of the things Brita had done with me, but I couldn't bear to mention them. He smiled and then put the tips of his fingers on my lips, light as a feather. He moved them back and forth across my lips, and it tickled terribly. I laughed. But at the same time it made me awfully horny. He put his hand on one of my breasts and took the tip of it between his fingers. He did it so gently that I almost didn't feel it. Then he let go of the nipple but left the palm of his hand there, all warm and still. Little by little, he let his hand brush slowly back and forth. I wanted to touch him under his white coat, but I didn't dare. Now he began to massage my nipple again, harder and harder until it was on the brink of hurting a little. He stopped and started over again just as cautiously as before. My nipple got red and swollen and stood out rigidly. Suddenly he bent over and took my other nipple in his mouth and began licking it ever so gently. Then he bit it tenderly and the sucking got stronger. He stopped a couple of times and started carefully over again. This brought both breasts to life, red and full of that lovely tingly feeling. I expected him to do something else now, but he just waited a moment and then continued to work on my breasts. I think he kept at them for ten minutes. Then he stopped.

"Sit up," he said. I got up and sat in front of him on the table.

"How do you feel?" he asked softly.

My head felt warm, and I was breathing hard. All I wanted was for him to keep going with me, either sucking my breasts again or doing something else still more lovely. I felt all choked up and had difficulty answering his question.

"Fine, thanks," was all I could manage. He smiled but didn't do a thing except hold one breast gently in his hand, from underneath as if he were holding a fruit.

"Do you feel like anything in particular now?" he asked, as coolly as if we were sitting in a restaurant talking about what to eat and he wanted to know if there was something he could order for me.

"Oh!" I said out loud and lay down again, wishing only that he would touch me between my legs. Instead he skimmed lightly over my front, beginning at my breasts, moving over my navel, and then down to the hair of my flower. Again and again. It began to hurt a little around there, and I felt the muscles and nerves in my abdomen tensing up. But he didn't touch me between the legs. He used his other hand to stroke my head and face gently. It felt as if my hair were electrified, and my scalp tingled. Every touch of his fingertips went like a little stab through my whole body.

Suddenly he said, "Have you gotten wet in the crotch yet?"

I couldn't say a word until I'd cleared my throat. "I don't know," I lied.

Thank God, I thought, now he's got to examine it for himself. Just once anyway!

"Feel for yourself," he said coolly.

Feeling like a hypocrite, I reached down between my thighs. Everything was slippery and squishy. I held my wet hand right up to his face so he couldn't miss the smell of the dampness.

"Yes," I said, "I guess it is getting a tiny bit wet."

"The reflexes there seem to be in order," said Dr. Peterson, and he got up. "Turn over on your stomach."

I turned over and lay with my bare bottom exposed. I thought of Brita and hoped he'd do something similar with me from behind. Although I wanted most for him to explore me in front, it wouldn't do any harm back there either. A moment went by, and I shyly lifted my backside to remind him of it as discreetly as I could. I tried to twist it a little, sort of wave it.

"No," Dr. Peterson said. "Just relax. Lie quietly."

I put my stomach and my mount down against the table again. He leaned over me and put both hands under my chest so that he held one breast in each hand. Suddenly I felt something that made me draw in my breath with a loud gasp. He had put his wet, warm mouth right against the nape of my neck. I gulped and began to squirm. His mouth slipped slowly down between my shoulder blades, then back up to the hairline of my neck. He repeated that several times. Then he released his grip under me and gave me a long, wet kiss on the small of my back. I felt it go straight through my stomach, and I couldn't hold still. He continued licking me, but farther down, from the small of my back down to the little triangle where my backside begins to divide in two. Then back up. Again and again. All at once he pushed his hand underneath me, down below. I held my breath and realized that I was clutching my hair with both hands. But he didn't do anything. He didn't move a finger, just kept his hand there. I knew his hand must be soaking wet, because I was slippery both between my legs and behind, since I'd lain on my back first. The kissing on the small of my back and down toward my behind was almost more than I could stand, but I sobbed out when he stopped it. Next he took one of my feet and put his mouth against the sole, which made me shudder in every muscle up to my eyebrows, but I managed to hold the foot still. He did the same thing with the other foot, and after that with the backs of my knees, which didn't feel so bad either. Then he let up for a while.

"Raise your seat a bit," he said, and I put it up in the air, while he pushed his left hand in under me in front and placed the right one on my back, by the buttocks, and pushed me down against the table. Now he had one hand in front and the other behind. My heart stood still with joy. But he didn't do what I was hoping for. Instead he started in with a sort of massage, which made my abdomen loosen up; he moved his right hand in circles, drawing my pelvis around with it, so that the outside of my flower got rubbed and rubbed against the hand that he had under me. It came close to hurting, because I had no sign that he would go into me, either in front or in back.

"Now," I thought, "now he's *got* to begin!"

He stopped abruptly and pulled his hands away.

"You may sit up," he said and just stood looking at me.

I got up and sat with my arms around my knees, resting my chin on them. I knew that I had left a damp spot under me on the white sheet. He looked at it too.

"All your external reflexes are completely in order," said Dr. Peterson and went back to his desk and sat down. "I find no disturbances whatever."

I felt dizzy and groggy, sitting there with my mouth open and my eyes as wet as my crotch was. My body was burning, and I had a feeling inside my sex that was enough to drive you crazy, half pain and half longing. "It just can't be possible," I thought. "He isn't going to stop now."

"The external examination is over. You may get dressed."

He glanced up at me, and I suppose I must have

looked a little strange, because he added, "Is anything wrong?"

I couldn't utter a word, but just ran my tongue around my half-open mouth and tried to push the hair back from my forehead.

"Is there something you want? Would you like something in particular?"

I was about to ask him to go on with the massaging and this time concentrate between my legs, but the minute I cleared my throat I thought of my mother. Her face rose before me. Oh God, what would she have said! What would she and grandmother have said if they saw the family's hope for the future, just eighteen years old, sitting naked on a doctor's table with a wet spot under her bottom and asking a stranger if he'd be kind enough to rub her between the legs? I couldn't make a sound. The thought of mother and grandmother paralyzed me, but it didn't affect my desire in the least.

"Then there's nothing you want," said Dr. Peterson and wrote a few more words on my file card.

I got up my courage and thought of a way to ask him in an indirect and more proper fashion. "Excuse me," I said, "but is the whole examination finished already?"

"Shall I continue?" he said.

I shut my eyes.

"Yes," I said softly and quite pathetically. He got up and came over to my table.

Placing a large pillow behind me, he said, "Lean back, but keep your legs in the same position."

I lay down with the pillow under my neck, holding my feet apart and my knees up, so that my flower was wide-open to view.

He didn't seem to notice it, since he started up by taking one of my breasts in his mouth again. That made things go from bad to worse. But then it finally happened.

He put his face between my legs, with his mouth against the sensitive skin on the inside of my thigh. He began at the middle of the thigh, kissing and licking slowly upward. Finally he all but fastened himself to me by sucking at the very top of my thigh, just by the abdomen where the skin is as thin as silk. He stuck out his tongue and licked me with small movements around the spot that is covered with light, soft hair. Now my abdomen was wet, as well as those parts of my groin that weren't already damp from before. It tingled through my stomach and my back and up through my body to my neck and my eyes. He used his mouth and fingers at the same time, and I could feel the honey running from my flower. I tossed my head back and forth and thought no more about mother. All at once I gave a cry. He spread my knees as far apart as he could and gave me a firm wet kiss between the two openings of my crotch. I thought I'd go crazy for sure. He pressed hard with his tongue, licking deep between my legs. It couldn't have been easy for him, because I just couldn't manage to hold still. Tears ran down my cheeks, and I mumbled words that I didn't understand myself. Suddenly he stopped and got up.

"All of your reflexes are functioning properly and soundly."

"No," I said.

"No?" he repeated. "Was there something wrong?"

"I . . . I . . . no . . . I . . ." I answered, giving him a pleading look.

"Is there something in particular you want?" he repeated as precisely as before.

Mama's picture was pretty faint now, but somewhere or other it was watching me, and I couldn't say what I wanted to.

"All right," he said, "then we're finished."

"Don't go away!" I pleaded.

"If there's something you want me to do," he said, "you have to tell me now. Say what it is!"

I summoned all my strength and said, "Can't you put your finger in my crotch?" I could hear how weak and pathetic my voice sounded.

"Where do you mean?" he asked coolly. "You have two places."

"In front," I said. "I'd like it best in front."

He put his hand over my sex, resting it there a moment. Then he pressed the opening shut and began to rub the edges lightly against each other. It was heavenly, and I had to gasp for air. He inserted one finger a short way into the slit itself and moved it gently back and forth. Fire ran through my veins, and I could feel my abdomen getting warm and hard; the muscles twitched in a sort of spasm. All at once he stuck his longest finger deep into me, and I gave out with a long sob. He pulled it in and out, and it was best when he didn't leave it in too long. He touched me on the clitoris, and I must say that *he* had no trouble finding it. After just a few seconds I was nothing but a wet, trembling lump. My body, my brain, and my face had all turned to jelly, and so had my stomach and the tips of my fingers. Heat ran through my abdomen, and I realized that something was coming that had never before happened to me with a man. I pulled my knees higher up and dug my fingers into my leg muscles. He put his face down in my crotch again with his mouth on my sex. He licked up and down several times, then took my clitoris in his mouth and massaged it with his lips and tongue. Right then I came, and I dug my fingers into his hair. It was strong and lasted a good while, with me lying there twisting, squirming, and screaming. The lovely part of it was that he didn't stop, but kept right on through my whole orgasm and for a good while afterward, except he worked a bit more slowly and gently after it was over.

When he stopped and got up, I was really finished. Yes, I was finished in every way. I was perspiring, damp, happy and warm, nothing but lovely, soft, and tired flesh. I didn't stop to think that he hadn't had an orgasm. It didn't even occur to me.

He went back to his desk.

"Well?" he said. "How are you now?"

"Wonderful!" I said gratefully, lying there naked and relaxed on the table.

"Fine," said Dr. Peterson. "Then there's nothing at all wrong with any of your physical reactions; they're all sound and effective, and as far as I can tell, stronger than with most women. Therefore it's purely psychic inhibitions that are causing you trouble and keeping you from achieving climaxes."

He picked up a pad and a ball-point pen and came

over to me. This time he sat down on a chair next to my table.

"Just lie as you are," he said. "We'll talk best when you have nothing on."

I found it pleasant and natural myself, since I wasn't particularly embarrassed with him any more. He knew my whole body quite well by now anyway. It's remarkable what a professional can do, I thought, and I smiled at him.

"I don't think we'll have any trouble with this problem. In a couple of months I believe you'll be able to have orgasms in the usual way, and quickly and easily at that. But we have to move carefully— little by little."

"I think I can manage it already," I said.

"No," he said emphatically, "you can't. You've got to get used to it gradually. Just one unsuccessful experiment now can ruin the whole treatment. If I'm going to carry on an effective treatment, you mustn't have anything to do with men for as long as you're under my care. If you don't observe that rule, I'll have to stop treating you immediately."

I solemnly promised him that I wouldn't have anything to do with other men until the treatment was over and I was well.

"Your trouble," continued Dr. Peterson, "is nothing more, in my opinion, than that you're full of anxiety and shame. You're crammed full of other people's bad consciences and guilt feelings, disguised under prettier names, like 'bashfulness' or 'shyness.' And whenever you've had anything to do with boys, these guilt feelings have ruined the pleasure in it for you.

You've lost faith in your ability to achieve a climax with them, and that in turn has made you all the more anxious about everything. Many young girls have the same problem, but naturally they don't know about it themselves. That's one side of the case, what we can call the principal cause. An effect of this 'conscience' or guilt feeling is that one comes to think much too much about oneself, so that when one is with someone else, one thinks of oneself as playing the leading role. One thinks only of oneself and of one's own pleasure. So we see that shame and guilt feelings—shyness, that is to say—lead to an egotism that destroys all pleasure, both for one's partner and for oneself. Do you follow me?"

"Yes . . . well . . . maybe not completely," I answered.

"We'll come back to it again," he said. He kept on for a time, posing questions and making notes in his pad. After a while, I began to feel like more treatment, but I didn't dare say so, and my appointment was over. We made a new appointment for the next day, while he made some notes at his desk.

Finally he said, "That will be just twenty crowns. The rest comes out of your government health insurance."

I had to smile, thinking what good use was being made of the tax-payers' money.

As I walked home, I felt a little weak in the knees.

All that night, and through the next morning and afternoon, I looked forward to my second treatment from Dr. Peterson, but as I stood outside his office door and rang the bell, I felt embarrassed and afraid. Earlier in the day, I had gotten a bit damp down below from thinking about the examination, and now I felt ashamed of myself.

He walked ahead of me into the office.

"Strip only below the waist," he said.

He sat down and watched me, and when I had taken off my shoes and stockings, I began to undo my slacks around the waist. As I pulled the zipper, I felt myself getting red as a beet, and I didn't dare look at him. I could hardly bear to think of all the things he'd done to me the day before. I took my slacks and panties off very slowly, looking at the floor the whole time. Strangely enough, it felt much more embarrassing to be naked from just the waist down.

"Oh yes," he said. "Now we know what we've got to do first of all. As long as you're ashamed of having a backside and sex organs, you'll never be able to enjoy yourself or other people."

"I was very embarrassed yesterday too," I said, "but I made the grade anyway. That was the first time I managed it with a man."

"No," he answered. "*You* didn't manage it. *I* managed it for you. Someday you've got to manage it without a specialist. Come here."

He was sitting on an ordinary office chair, and when I came over to him he took me by the waist and sat me down astride his lap, with my face toward him. I began to enjoy it, but at the same time I was frightened, and I trembled a little. For a while I just sat there waiting, naked below the waist. He touched me gently on my hairs and played with them.

"Lillian," he said suddenly "do you get an orgasm when you masturbate?"

"What?" I said.

"You come when you're alone by yourself, don't you?"

I nodded.

"How do you go about it?" He looked at me calmly and attentively. I didn't answer.

"Tell me exactly how you do it! There's nothing to be ashamed of, and it's quite a common thing. You're not the only person in the world who gets pleasure from that sort of thing. Just what do you do with yourself?"

"I do it with my fingers," I said. "I just rub myself in front with my fingers, on the very outside where . . . where . . . you used your mouth and your tongue at the end yesterday."

Now I noticed that I was beginning to warm up from sitting on his lap, and I really wanted to feel him, to see if he'd gotten long and stiff.

"Show me how you go about it," he said.

I swallowed and bit my tongue carefully.

"I won't be able to make it if you're watching," I said.

"Do it anyway."

I looked down and put my hand to my slit, where I began to rub gently with my index finger. He took me under the chin and turned by face toward him.

"Look me in the eye while you do it," he said.

I looked him in the eye and went on working on myself, wondering why in the world he didn't want to do it with me. It was truly strange to sit opposite a man and do something like that. In a way it was nice, because my anxiety was gone, and I felt sure of him. He nimbly unbuttoned my shirt, my breasts came out, and he took a nipple between the thumb and forefinger of each hand, rubbing them in that special way of his. It felt good now, and I straightened my back as I kept on playing with myself. I knew I could never come that way, but it was great anyway. He let go of my breasts and unexpectedly reached behind me, stroking me above the rear and up past the small of my back. He pushed me back, put his face to my stomach, and kissed me for a long time on the navel. I forgot to finger myself.

Then he raised his head and looked me in the eye.

"You were ashamed and had a guilty conscience over what I did with you yesterday. Were you ashamed of enjoying it?"

"Yes," I said softly, nodding.

"You thought you'd done something wrong?"

"Yes—that's how I felt."

"Doing something wrong means hurting others, doing them harm, doesn't it?"

"Yes," I said. I felt calm now and was glad to be back with Dr. Peterson. He put his hand under my crotch and scratched me gently and beautifully back and forth.

"If you had disliked what I did with you yesterday, you wouldn't have a guilty conscience about it, would you?"

He let a finger stop at the place between the two openings and tickled me carefully. My legs shuddered. At the same time, he put another finger inside me in front, just a tiny bit, and moved it around.

I answered in a kind of fog, "That's right. Then it wouldn't have made any difference."

"Well," he said, continuing to work slowly and easily on my crotch, "what you liked and what gave you pleasure must then have harmed someone. Whom did you harm by having an orgasm yesterday?"

"I don't know," I said.

I felt funny, because I was following both what he was saying and what he was doing between my legs. One of his fingers slipped over my clitoris and massaged it lightly as a feather.

"Come on," he said, "*who* was hurt because *you* had a good time?"

My clitoris responded all-out to his fingers, and I hoped he'd take a little stronger hold of it. I was beginning to feel loose throughout my body.

"Just think if mama had seen me!" slipped out of me, and with that I began to laugh. Dr. Peterson smiled.

"Imagine if mama could see you now!" he said. "For she doesn't have the same things under her dress at all, does she? And she never has, has she?"

I laughed, and I could feel how his skillful fingers were working me back into a state of bliss. Then he stopped.

"Turn around," he said tersely.

I turned around and sat the same way—straddling his lap, but with my back to him.

"Bend over forward," he said in a more friendly way, "and put the palms of your hands on the floor. Way out in front of you."

I bent all the way down and could feel him pulling my legs farther out to the sides, so that my crotch opened to him. I was a little embarrassed again, but I also felt a tickling and titillating sensation in my abdomen and rear. He put his hand under my stomach from behind and continued his work. It was strange about this position, though, and at first I didn't see the point. Then came the explanation.

My bottom must have been wide open, because my legs were stretched far out, and suddenly I felt his mouth against the inside of my buttocks. Then he put his mouth all the way in. Everything between my legs was starting to melt, in front and in back. It didn't last nearly long enough. He stopped.

"Are you embarrassed now?" he said.

"No," I said and tried to turn my face up to him.

"All right," he continued, "you may go over and lie down on the table."

I walked over and lay down on my side, so I could look at him. I still had my shirt on over my shoulders, but open in front. I took it off while I was lying there. He smiled. I waited impatiently for him to come over and resume his examination of my reflexes. He walked slowly over to the table and sat down beside me.

"Well," he said, "what do you feel like doing now?"

All at once I felt like doing something new. I was dying to see his pecker and his testicles. I wondered how they looked and if he was any bigger than Henry. But the minute I wanted to say so, I couldn't. I thought right away of mother and grandmother. And I was afraid Dr. Peterson might not like the idea. Instead I took my breasts in my hands as if I wanted to give them to him.

"Oh yes," he said, "we've neglected them today. They'll get what's coming to them."

He put one hand on my abdomen while he took my breasts in his mouth, one after the other, deeply and for a long time. His hand pushed past my flower and on down between my legs. I wanted him to move it up again. And he did, but much too gently. Then he stopped.

"You and Brita had a lot of fun together," he said. "What did you like best?"

I felt calm and happy, and very horny—I was good and wet between the legs, and I thought of some things Brita had done with me.

"She used to take my temperature every so often," I said. That was good. "Then she'd play with me in front at the same time."

"You mean she'd take your temperature under your arm?"

"No," I said and laughed. "She stuck it into me in back."

I turned my back to him and pulled by buttocks apart with my fingers.

"There!" I said.

"And that was very good?"

"It was wonderful!"

At that I noticed I had been talking to him without feeling embarrassed and without giving my mother or grandmother a thought. And this after only one previous treatment. But I wasn't ashamed now, because there was a good, warm sensation running through my body, and I wanted him to do something to me to make that good feeling get stronger and stronger. He had noticed it too, for his hand moved into my crotch as though in answer.

"See?" he said. "You're getting there! Shall I do the same thing for you?"

"Please do," I said, hoping he'd begin.

One of his fingers penetrated deep into my flower, and it was lovely. But he pulled it out as soon as it was wet.

"Lie down on your back and pull your knees up," he said.

I did so, and he carefully inserted his finger deep into the opening in back. It was a strange feeling, which hurt a little, but a very good one. Then he put his mouth on my stomach and began to lick me from the navel down. Slowly, ever so slowly, while he lightly brushed a finger of his free hand over the outer opening of my flower, then took my clitoris gently between two fingers. That was all he moved, his fingers, and by now it was pouring out of me. My body jerked into motion and I just couldn't lie still any longer. It was pure heaven and past all under-standing—I could tell that I was going to have an orgasm again today, even if my head wasn't clear enough to have any more really conscious thoughts.

I tingled from the soles of my feet up through my spine, and the skin tightened at the nape of my neck. But apart from that, all my feelings came together below my stomach. I kept thinking that *now,* now I was going to come! But the awful part was that every time I approached a climax, he stopped moving his fingers and just held them inside me, one behind and the other in front. At times the desire was so strong that I had the impression I was lifting my feet over my head. The muscles in my stomach were tensing by themselves, and down in my seat and my thighs—and inside my abdomen as well as in my crotch between the two openings he was working so skillfully on—I could feel the muscles tensing and relaxing in a regular rhythm. One two, one two . . . But every time the high point and moment of deliverance approached, his fingers grew still, and there I was, back on solid ground again.

In the midst of all this, I had a shock. He released his grip in front and let my clitoris alone.

Then I thought I'd go crazy. He had put his mouth into my crotch again. It felt just as if some warm, living creature was on its way inside me. He opened his mouth around my whole flower, and sucked. His tongue slid up to my clitoris and hot, mad waves rushed through me. Then he stopped. Neither the finger in my backside nor his mouth against my flower did anything. I just felt warm breath in my crotch and against my hair and up along the bottom part of my stomach.

When I had calmed down a bit, and things had let up for me, he started in again—cautiously, slowly, almost unnoticeably. I don't know how many times he repeated this, but I was going crazy.

Suddenly he stopped altogether. He took his mouth away and pulled his finger, quickly and coldly, almost brutally, out of my rectum. I started crying and noticed that I could taste salt on my face. It took me a while before I could look at him. He was sitting quite unmoved beside me and making notes in his pad.

I was completely beside myself.

He'd kept me right on the brink of an orgasm the

whole time, probably for twenty minutes—and now he was sitting there writing.

I could only think about what else I might have him do.

Actually, I knew very well what I wanted.

I was flushed, out of breath, and sweaty. My body was hot and my heart beat much more strongly than usual. I had to wait before I could speak.

"Dr. Peterson . . . ?" was all I managed.

He didn't even raise his head. "Is there something wrong?" he asked and wrote on.

"Yes," I said, but my voice failed me again.

"Yes?"

He turned his head and looked deep into my eyes. After a moment he changed. He came down to earth again, and suddenly smiled.

"Is there anything you feel like doing?"

"Uhh . . ." I said, "Uh . . ."

"Speak up! Tell me exactly what you want."

I turned to him and took his hand. He put the pad away.

"Tell me what it is. Say what you want."

I looked at his white coat. He was wearing light khaki trousers under it, but apparently had nothing else on.

"Are you a . . . man?" I asked.

"Yes," he said. "A man of science. First of all, I want to help you, and secondly collect evidence, statistical evidence, on young women's orgasmic inhibitions. I'm planning a work of great impact for gynecological psychiatry. That's my field, you know."

These were the first words he'd ever said about himself.

"But," I said, "don't you get worked up, don't you get horny, when you treat—well, me, for example— that way?"

"Of course!" he said and a moment later added, "But I'm interested in *you,* not in myself. You're the one who's being helped."

I let my hand slip down against the bottom button of his white coat.

"Don't you get . . . don't . . . doesn't it get stiff on you?"

"What?" he said. "What do you mean by *it?*"

I half shut my eyes and smiled at him without showing my teeth. It was wonderful to speak intimately with him.

"Your thing. Your pecker."

"Oh yes," he said, "stiff as a board. Is there something you want?"

I abandoned all thought of mother and grandmother.

"Yes," I said. "I want to see your sex."

"Then you can find it for yourself," he said.

I blushed again, but it didn't make any difference, since the thought that he was going to let me see it went through my body like a flash of lightning.

"Stand up!" I said and rolled partly on one side. "Now it's *my* turn to be doctor for a while. Stand just like that!"

His fly was on a level with my face. I unbuttoned his white coat. Underneath was the waist of his trousers, and I saw instantly that there was something in his pants. I undid his fly. He had on tight tricot undershorts. It proved to be impossible to get that big stiff thing out through the opening in his shorts, so I took hold of the shorts and jerked them down to about the middle of his thighs.

I got dizzy the moment I'd done it. His organ stood stiff and straight out. It was quite a bit bigger then Henry's, and right away I thought, "It's too big! You'll never manage to get it into you." It was longer than Henry's and much thicker. But it was beautiful, and up front the head was purple or dark red in color. Back by the root he had a lot of dark hair— not sprinkled with gray like at his temples. I felt a maddening desire to bite at it or take it in my mouth. It loomed there on a level with my own head. I pushed forward on the table and put the end of it between my breasts. I squeezed my breasts against it, and then I couldn't resist any longer. I moved my face nearer and nearer to it, rubbed my cheek against it, and after that my lips. I kissed it. That seemed to make it get bigger still—or in any case just as hard as iron. I kissed it several times.

"Well?" said Dr. Peterson. "Was that all?"

It took all the courage I had just to think the thought.

"Can you try . . . to . . . do you think . . . that it . . . ?" I was thinking that it was surely too big for my flower, that it would never fit where God without a doubt had meant it to be.

"Try what?" he said.

I put my hands in my crotch and raised my bottom from the table.

"You know what I mean."

"All right," he said, "all right."

He walked to the foot of the wheeled table, took me by the ankles, and pulled me down. Then he put my legs up in those strange supports. The metal was cold under the backs of my knees. But I could hardly breathe any more.

"Actually it's too soon," said Dr. Peterson, "but I'll do it anyway. Push the pillow up under your neck so you can see part of what goes on."

I followed his instructions, and I could see my soft white stomach and his powerful dark manliness just beyond my separated thighs.

Quite deliberately he put the tip to the opening of my sex, then placed his right thumb against my clitoris and began to massage it gently. He pushed his pecker more firmly against my opening, so I began to feel what it was, and then put it in about half an inch. I gulped for air. It was much bigger than Henry's, but it didn't hurt. It stretched me a little, that's all. He kept on massaging my clitoris, and the whole thing seemed to catch on fire. Then he pushed in. Now it did hurt a bit, but it was slipping in. I reached down and felt for it. The head was in me now. He held it still and kept rubbing with his fingers. I twisted like a snake.

He pushed it a bit farther in, about two inches, but all the time he kept up his work on my clitoris with the tip of his thumb. Then he pressed himself slowly in the whole way, and I could feel my sex opening around him. It closed him in. It held him tight. It was the first time I'd had a male organ in me and actually *liked* it. He kept up the massaging while he slowly pulled his sex out of mine. He held it far out, then inserted it again. He kept on. Slowly, then quickly. Everything seemed like an enormous wave to me. Like a big tree that kept falling and falling and falling. The movement of his thumb merged with the movement of his pecker inside me. I stretched myself into an arc from my bottom to my neck. I could have wrapped my legs around his neck and choked him. I started to come. He kept right on with his penis, slowly in and out, in and out—at the same time working on my clitoris with his fingers. I was coming and I screamed out loud. I covered my face with my hands and shouted. It hit my whole abdomen. Ten times stronger than with Brita. My head felt swollen and filled with cotton, almost numb. I didn't know my own name. I just twisted, raised my back from the table, and screamed. I howled. My middle melted, along with my legs down to my knees, my stomach, my back, my breasts, my mouth—all of them were in on it.

He didn't lose his composure for a single second. When he knew I was coming full force, he kept on working gently with his thumb, holding his pecker inside me without moving. Not until my climax was almost over did he let go with his hand and lean forward, pulling his organ almost out and thrusting it back in, again and again. I noticed this in spite of my ecstasy and even though I was shaking over my whole body. Then suddenly he lay down on me full weight, pushed his pecker deep inside me, and that crazy, warm fluid gushed into me. My whole orgasm seemed to be happening again, but in a different way.

I lowered my head on the pillow and saw his head against my chest. My right hand burrowed in his hair and patted him. And everything disappeared in a warm, peaceful haze.

He lay on top of me for a good while with his

pecker inside me. But now it was soft and supple. It was just as well he lay there like that; the echoes lasted a long time.

I may have gone to sleep for a few minutes.

When I opened my eyes, conscious again, he was sitting beside me on the table, holding my hand.

"Is there anything you want?" he said.

I smiled.

"What in the world could I possibly want?"

"Wait just a minute," he said, "I have a kitchen here. And where there's a kitchen, there's a refrigerator."

He went out and in a minute came back with a champagne bottle in his hand. In his other hand he had two tall, thin glasses. His penis hung down quietly and well-behaved, like a pendulum. He opened the bottle, and it popped.

With his hand lying peacefully in my lap, we toasted my first successful encounter with a man.

"But," he said, "you mustn't think for a minute that everything's all right yet. You've got to get used to it and feel secure about it. Relaxation is the thing. At the same time, you mustn't get dependent on me. You must have complete confidence in yourself, and get rid of both your shame and your guilty conscience. When you showed up today, you really looked pathetic."

"Yes," I nodded.

"You'll have an appointment again tomorrow," he went on. "It's important that it happen every day. But I can't spend so much time with you in the weeks ahead. Once in a while it'll only be ten minutes."

My heart jumped with joy when I heard that it was going to go on every day for weeks ahead. That sounded fine.

We quietly drank up the champagne, while he held his fingers in the narrow, damp slit between my legs. Little by little he began to move them, and I felt my desire returning. He kept at it in the slit, up and down, up and down. It was lovely again, but he seemed to be lost in thought. All of a sudden he looked me in the eye.

"You're still embarrassed," he said. "You're even embarrassed with me, a doctor. With anyone else, you'd be just as inhibited as before."

"I'm not embarrassed with you," I said, raising my knees and stretching them open as far as I could. I put both hands down to the opening and pulled the edges out to the sides.

"There!" I said. "Am I embarrassed?"

He kept his fingers just inside me, and his thumb moved over my clitoris. The tingling was getting strong now, and I took a look at his pecker. It was throbbing slightly, and gradually it rose up, big, stiff, and thick. I thought how I had just had the whole thing inside me, and it struck me how much stretch there really was to that narrow little opening of mine once it got heated up to the boiling point. I felt like having his pecker in me again, so I put my hand around it and pulled the skin back and forth over the shiny, swelling head. I could see it was having an effect on him, and his fingers moved faster between my legs.

He stopped and got up. "Time's up."

"Oh no," I said. "Can't you do it once more?"

"We're not here for the fun of it," he answered. "The government's paying for it."

"Don't stop now," I pleaded. "Please."

"Anything I do with you must have a purpose. Basically you're still embarrassed, and that embarrassment must be eliminated before you can relax and not tie yourself up in knots."

I suspected that he had something in mind that might not be so much fun as what I'd been hoping for. He thought for a moment, then raised his head and pointed to a door.

"In there," he said, "is a sort of washroom. There's an enema kit hanging on the wall. Go out there, fill it up with soapy lukewarm water, and bring it back here full. Then lie down on the table again."

My face turned red. "No," I said. "No."

"If you don't do as I say, I'll end the treatment immediately. In that case there'll be no appointment tomorrow."

I knew that he meant what he said, but I thought it would be terribly embarrassing to be given an enema. Especially by him.

"Do I *have* to?"

"Have to what?" he said. He was putting his white coat back on. There I stood, naked and embarrassed, with my cheeks flaming red and my hair hanging down over my forehead.

"Do I have to take an enema?" I asked weakly. I felt such a mess.

"Yes, you do," he said, "and you're going out and get it ready yourself."

I saw that pleading would do me no good, so I walked over and opened the door to the bathroom. It looked as much like a laboratory as a bathroom, with different kinds of apparatus, like flasks, glassware, and syringes. I somehow felt that the room belonged to a gynecologist. On the wall hung a huge enema bag and all that went with it—the rubber hose and the black tip that was soon to be stuck into my rear.

I took the bag down and went over to the basin, in which I placed a bar of soap and turned on the hot water. I felt so pathetic, standing there fixing the enema that was to be used for my own humiliation and exposure. I say "exposure," though I had nothing against an enema itself. In fact I rather liked enemas, but only when I was alone and knew that no one could see me. The thought that Dr. Peterson might discover this was enough to make me scream. But I went through with it, knowing that otherwise he would break off the treatments, and after these first two appointments I wouldn't do without them for anything.

I stirred up the water; the temperature was right, and it was soapy. I took out the bar of soap, still blushing and feeling embarrassed, and walked out to Dr. Peterson with the thing in my hand. He was sitting at his desk, but he got up and took it from me. I couldn't bear to look at him, but just stared at the floor with my back hunched over.

"Thank you," he said.

"You're welcome," I said, curtsying weakly.

The awful thing was that my body below the waist

was looking forward to what was going to happen. But I could have died from shame anyway. I turned around and sneaked over to the table, where I lay down on my stomach.

"How shall I lie?" I asked bitterly.

"However you like best," he said. "But you've forgotten something I'm sure you always remember otherwise."

"What's that?"

"Come here, and I'll show you what I mean."

I got up and walked across the floor with my head bowed. On his desk was a vasoline jar.

"You forgot to smear some vasoline on the tip," he said. "And also on yourself. You've got to have a little vasoline in your backside."

I put some vasoline on my finger without looking at him and rubbed it on the tip. He held the jar out again, and I took some more vasoline on my right index finger. At that moment he took me by the chin and turned my face up to his.

"Look this way," he said. "Now you can grease yourself in back."

With my left hand I opened my buttocks and put the blob of vasoline in, outside the opening.

"No," he said. "You haven't put your finger in, have you? That's the best way."

Just as I got my finger in, he kissed me on the mouth, and a pillar of flame shot through me. I walked over to the wheeled table, and he followed me with the enema in his hand. I lay on my back with my knees way up.

"Is that the way you're used to doing it yourself?" he asked.

He *did* know then, and I turned beet red once again. But my backside, my abdomen, and my stomach started aching with desire and tension. He took my legs and set them up in the supports. I lay waiting to feel the tip go in me. Instead he bent down and kissed me on my flower, which had opened up a little while I was waiting. I could tell that I was altogether wet from my own slippery fluid, so wet in fact that I didn't need vasoline. He licked my clitoris until I began squirming, then stopped completely. A moment later I felt the tip go in, but only a tiny bit. He began massaging my clitoris as the tip was pushed farther and farther in. I grew terribly excited and wanted to squeeze my legs together. I saw him far off, in a kind of haze, as he opened his white coat in front and revealed his spear in all its splendor.

Now the tip stayed in my little opening by itself, and he lifted the bag with one hand and worked on my clitoris with the other. When I felt the warm water coming up inside me, I began crying aloud. It was so unspeakably lovely that I took hold of both sides of the table to keep myself still. It was then I noticed he had put his sex up to my slit and was pressing it in. He began moving it quite slowly, mostly at the very outer edge, but every now and then inside me. All this time the water was coming in my backside, and his free hand kept massaging my clitoris. I clung to the table and gave out a loud scream while the tears flowed down my cheeks. I started coming in huge, shaking convulsions, but he kept right on as if nothing were happening. Not until I was almost finished did he pour his own load into me, so that I was getting it from both directions at once. When we were both through, he kept on with the rest of the enema, which I still didn't mind a bit.

After a while he finished.

I lay like jelly on the table, almost unconscious. My body felt soft and slack and lovely, all warm and relaxed. My insides were full of water—and that felt good too. But the trouble was that I had to go out to the toilet again. I rolled down off the table and stood weak and dizzy on the floor, completely happy, but almost unable to walk, my knees were so weak. In a way, I was still coming inside. I staggered toward his bathroom.

"Shall I come along," he said, "and watch?"

"Yes, please," I said and smiled. I understood why he had given me the enema, which had revealed me deep down inside. Now I had no secrets from him, and I felt as safe and secure as a little child when I looked at him. I took his hand and held it against my cheek as we went in. I sat down on the toilet and emptied myself.

It's a marvelous feeling, to have nothing to hide.

Now I had complete confidence in him, and I could put myself in his hands without worrying about exposing myself or being silly or stupid. I wasn't even embarrassed any more about liking to have an enema.

From now on I could tell him everything, all about myself and all my secrets.

He said just one thing: "Remember, no unsuccessful experiments with men so long as you're under treatment." Those were easy orders to follow; I didn't want anyone but him.

I graduated from school that year, with honors. I was weakest in math, but good in languages, and I got my best grades in composition. That's the way it's always been.

3

I continued with Dr. Peterson about every day for a couple of months, but it wasn't always like the first two appointments. He was often pressed for time and could give me only a few minutes. But that didn't matter, because I was well prepared by the time I arrived. While on the way to his office, I would start getting damp in the crotch, and by the time I stood in front of his door I was dripping wet down there. Soon it was enough just to think about him.

On those days when time was short, I would just walk in, say hello, and pull down my panties before I lay down, usually face down, on his examining table. The usual thing was for him to put his left hand between my legs, inside my slit, while he worked on the small of my back and my rear with the other hand. Once in a while he'd use his mouth. That way it was only a matter of minutes before I came, and I was always completely satisfied.

At times he'd be so busy that we hardly exchanged a word. But the treatments kept right on; every single day for two or three months I had a full-fledged orgasm.

I always decided for myself what I wanted whenever he didn't have time to give me a more thorough treatment. I would lie down on my back or on my stomach, according to what I felt like. It was lovely, too, to have his mouth in front, with his whole head between my legs.

Apart from this purely physical treatment, I got an endless series of questions on everything about me, my feelings, my childhood, and my parents. Quite often I couldn't understand what he was driving at with this probing. But it did have a purpose. One day something entirely new happened.

As I came in, he took me in his arms and kissed me on the mouth. We sat down fully clothed on his leather sofa, and he continued his warm, powerful kissing. He licked my lips and my ears, nibbled at my throat and the back of my neck, and then kissed me on the mouth again. I was now soaking wet in my pants.

Then we got up, undressed together, and soon were lying side by side on the table, without a stitch on. He had his arms around me, and our stomachs and chests touched. I could feel the point of his weapon against my thigh. He kissed me tenderly while he stroked my back. We lay there exactly like an ordinary pair of lovers, and it seemed so normal I almost felt embarrassed. For a moment I forgot he was treating me as a doctor, and felt as if I were having an affair with him. It was just beautiful! How lovely to lie there with him like that.

As he continued, it was more love play than treatment. He took my breast in his mouth, and the hand on my back slipped cautiously down and into the crevice between the half-moons. He didn't say a word, just licked my nipple. His other hand played with my hair. He pushed his knee between my legs to spread them apart. Then he began with the hand in front—he opened the damp slit and rubbed the inner lips with his fingers. After a while he rubbed just the clitoris, and switched to kissing me on the mouth—I felt as if my mouth and my flower were one and the same. He had turned into a lover instead of a doctor, and now he seemed almost like a boy.

Between my tongue and my sex was flowing a current of something I can't describe, a combination of delight, desire, and happiness. I turned part way over on my back and opened my legs wide. He came along and lay on top of me, first with his hard-as-steel pecker against my stomach. I turned all the way over on my back and pulled him down, so that I got his hot sex between my legs. I took hold of the head and massaged it before pushing it into the opening of my flower. He held it there, rubbing it against the lips.

"Come on," I said. "Now!"

He did as I said, first just barely in, then all the way. He did it gently and affectionately. Every so often he would lie still with his pecker inside me, our groins pressed together. Then he would pull it slowly out and put it quickly back in, or he might pull it quickly out and put it—oh so slowly—back in. Or he'd do something altogether different—hold it in halfway while he moved his hips from side to side or up and down. Sometimes he'd move them in a big circle, so I could feel his pecker moving inside me in all directions.

He was lying with the whole top half of his body on me, kissing me on the corners of my mouth, on my eyes, and all over my face. It was lovely to feel his body moving, and I began to fret and groan with each motion of his pecker. It worked ceaselessly, but never for long in the same way. Now almost every thrust was different and gave me a new feeling. Now and then it would be *almost* motionless, then would come a sudden, hard movement—he'd either pull it almost out or plunge it far in. I was beginning to scream and call out words without meaning, and I was hot and a little sweaty as the stream poured out of my opening and down under me. Then came spasms so powerful that I lifted the two of us right up off the table and screamed. My muscles tensed again and again, and I felt my abdomen melting and running out of me down where his enormous, slick pecker was at work. I came like a waterfall, and so did he, right along with me. With all his strength he grabbed me by my shoulders with both hands, biting me in the neck and pushing his sex deep into me, as the warm stream gushed from him and filled me. He stayed on me, warm and heavy, with his head against my shoulder and his pecker in where it belonged. I kept right on coming until I couldn't any more.

We lay that way for a long time, warm and peaceful, on a sort of gentle, lovely cloud. I floated along as if on a warm river, my body soft and tired.

I had never dreamed that ordinary, everyday intercourse could be so enormously lovely. I'm sure one of the reasons was that in that position our bodies came so close together, from head to toe, and that I felt the movements of his chest and stomach the whole time.

I ran my hand through his hair and kissed him on the cheek. It was like holding a child.

He raised his head and looked me in the eye. We smiled. He slowly pulled his organ out, and I moaned.

It had felt so good to have it in me even when it was relaxed and soft.

He got up. "Now I'll go out and pull another cork."

He brought a bottle and two tall, thin glasses from the kitchen. We laughed when the cork popped. He sat down beside me, both of us warm and a bit sweaty. We sipped togther at the cold, fresh champagne.

"That was your first time," he said. "Now you're grown up."

I knew he was right. That was the first time he'd made me come without using his finger on my clitoris at the same time he had his pecker working inside me.

I felt as though I were having an affair with him, even if, after all, I was still his patient and not his mistress.

He sat next to me as we drank, but one of his hands was lightly touching my flower. He looked at his watch.

"Well," he said, "our time is up now. You're due tomorrow at the same time, but I'm going to leave you with a little remembrance of me."

He took the champagne cork and played with it between his fingers and then rubbed it gently against my soft slit. He pushed it in very carefully, while I gasped for air. It gave me a feeling I'd never had before. He pushed it all the way in with his middle finger.

"Keep it there until tomorrow. Try to keep from taking it out."

I got up. The cork felt fine inside me. It didn't

hurt in the slightest. Anything but. I felt it constantly, as I got dressed and whenever I moved.

Before I left, he gave me a long kiss, as if I weren't a patient any more at all.

I had a night like nothing I've ever known before or since.

Not a second went by that I didn't feel the titillation of the champagne cork. Whether I was walking, standing, sitting, or lying down, there it was all the time, reminding me that I was a woman and not letting me forget what had happened at the office. All night long it kept me just as horny as if Dr. Peterson himself had been with me. I was sexually excited right out to the tips of my fingers and toes, and as time went by it got to be almost more than I could stand. I wondered if I was about to go crazy, and more than once I was all set to take it out. But I wanted to do all I could to follow Dr. Peterson's instructions to the letter. When I had gone to bed that evening, my hand went automatically down to my flower. I just couldn't help playing with myself. I took my clitoris in my fingers and played with it for probably not more than half a minute before I had an orgasm. It helped some, but after I'd read in bed for half an hour, I felt like doing it again. I didn't though—just to save everything for the next day.

Finally I went to sleep, but in the morning I had the impression that I'd had erotic dreams all night long. As I was taking my shower, the cork started up again with full force, and at breakfast I was completely beside myself. I couldn't manage to eat more than half a slice of bread with marmalade. Going to school was out of the question. I scratched myself like a madwoman, on my abdomen and all over my body, and while drinking my coffee I thought I might come on the spot. I ran out of the house to the first telephone booth I could find and called Dr. Peterson.

Luckily he was already at his office, and he let me come right up. I used the last of my pocket money to take a taxi, and I all but ran up the steps to his office.

In the office, I dashed up to him and threw my arms around his neck. For a while we stood kissing like the day before, then got undressed. He fished the cork out of me so quickly and easily that I hardly noticed it, and we lay down in the same way, pressed against each other, mouth to mouth. I could have eaten him up. I lasted that way for about two seconds before I turned over on my back and spread my legs. I was bursting, and had to hold onto the edges of the table.

"Come on," I said. "Quick!"

He did, and I screamed the minute his fat, throbbing pecker entered me. The tears streamed from my eyes, and I started coming immediately. I came in a huge black wave, and I squirmed so much that he had to grip me tightly. The wave came on so strong I think I fainted. I'm sure I was unconscious for a moment anyway. Then came the echo of the orgasm, but he wasn't finished yet. He continued as he had the day before, and while he was kissing me I realized I was coming again. It took a bit longer this time, but I came with full force at the same time he did. We lay as if woven together—tangled up with each other into one big lump. Then he sank down with his head on my breast and with his love organ still in me.

From then on he used the champagne cork every so often. But otherwise we went on like an ordinary couple in love, in the regular position, with me underneath and him on top, and always with the same result. We did it every single day for a couple of weeks.

It got to be a matter of course for me to get complete satisfaction in this normal way.

I felt healthy.

One day he had the bathtub filled when I arrived. We stood embracing as we did at the beginning of every treatment, but suddenly he said, "We're going to take a bath together today."

I looked up and smiled, for it sounded exciting, though I had trouble thinking that anything could be better than just lying with him in my arms.

We got undressed as usual, and his sex had already risen up in advance. He took me under the arm as we went into the bathroom.

I got into the tub first, and he leaned over me with a bar of fragrant bath soap in his hand. He dipped it in the water and rubbed it between his hands until it made big, soft suds. He began to wash my body, first my hands, neck, and feet, and then my legs up to my crotch. There he stopped. Then he washed my back, down to my bottom. His fingers went carefully in between the half-moons up at the top.

God, what supple, sensitive fingers that man had!

The washing began to take strong effect on me. He bathed my breasts—unbelievably slowly and carefully, and the nipples sprang to life. We were laughing and talking together the whole time. And his pecker was standing straight up.

Then he washed me around the backside, and I had to get up and bend over while he soaped inside the crevice, around the tight little opening. I turned my stomach toward him, and he soaped in front with the same care and consideration he had shown in back, until it started feeling warm inside my groin.

Afterward, he gave me a good, thorough rubbing with a towel, and at the very end he smeared a little skin oil on both my openings, making them soft and elastic. He rubbed oil into the place between them too, while I lay on the bath mat with my legs apart.

Then he got into the tub, and I started bathing him.

I didn't spend so much time on the top half of his body, since he was actually already nice and clean.

I went at it all the more thoroughly down below his navel, rubbing him time and again with soft, warm suds from the middle of his stomach down to the roots of that magnificent pecker of his. He didn't seem to object especially.

"Get up," I said.

He stood up in the tub with his pecker bulging at me. It looked even more red, dark, and wild set against the chalk-white suds that surrounded it. With the suds in my hand I began, so very, very enticingly, to bathe him between his legs. First at the top of the thighs, then much too carefully around his testicles. I let them rest in my hands as I rubbed on the suds, which I then rinsed off slowly by dripping water on him. Finally he was so clean he could hardly stand up. His penis jutted out red and stiff, like a lighthouse against the white suds. That dark tower had no suds on it at all.

I could see that he was waiting.

I rubbed the bar of soap between my hands to make more of the soft, sweet-smelling suds.

Light as a feather, I smoothed the suds onto his spear. He clutched at the wall. I took firmer hold of his organ and felt how unbelievably hard it was, just like steel under the soapsuds. He shuddered whenever I touched the shaft or the head of it. I washed it cautiously and tenderly. Very carefully in fact, to keep him from coming. I succeeded.

After I'd played with him for quite a while, I rinsed him off with lukewarm water.

"Get out," I said. "You're all wet."

He climbed out of the tub, and I could see that he was not himself. I used a large, rough bath towel to get him good and dry. When I rubbed his spear with the rough material, he doubled up. Now *I* was the one who was getting ideas.

When he was dry all the way down, I smeared some skin oil on the palms of my hands and between my fingers. I grabbed him firmly at the root of his pecker with my right hand and pulled my hand toward me until the head of his penis slipped from my grip. Right away I took hold with my left hand and again pulled my hand outward. I kept it up that way. It was the same kind of movement you use to milk a cow. But what a cow! A strong, handsome man with an M.D. and two certified specialties. When I closed my fingers around his powerful staff of love, I saw how small and thin my hands were next to that volcano.

I kept doing it just slowly enough to keep him from coming. He tensed like a steel spring. This time *he* was the one who didn't know his own name. Who couldn't speak. Who couldn't walk. Who just groaned and clutched at the wall.

All this time warm, slippery fluid ran from my flower and down the inside of my legs. If I'd had shoes and stockings on, they would have been soaking wet.

Anyway, he was the one who broke off the idyll.

He pulled his organ from me and turned away. "Come on!" he said after a moment, and walked back into the office.

I followed him, and he sat down at his desk.

I waited.

He lit a cigarette and blew the smoke in my direction. My abdomen was turning to melted butter, and I wished he'd get something going between the two of us.

But his pecker had gone down, and he looked calm, clearheaded, and deliberate. He was reflecting. Then he said, "Almost everyone ruins his sex life by thinking only of himself."

I was standing before him naked, and his words struck me hard. I knew what he meant, and I thought of what I'd done to Henry. I knew that the worst things about me were the feelings and concepts I'd been indoctrinated with by my mother and grandmother. Virtue, modesty, shame, guilt, anxiety—all were lies. I sat down across from him.

"Give me a cigarette," I said.

He handed me one, and I felt how healthy and good the smoke burned its way down to my lungs.

"*Denn alle Lust will Ewigkeit, will tiefe, tiefe Ewigkeit!*" he said softly, as if he were recalling a childhood lesson.

I understood enough German to know what he meant, but I didn't get the point of his saying it right then and there. We sat for a moment and smoked.

"Listen to me now," he said, "there are a couple of things I must tell you.

"People speak of 'sexual morality,' but that is a misleading expression. *There is no special morality for sex.* No matter what you do with yourself, whether you go to bed with girls or with boys, and no matter what it occurs to you to do with them or with yourself, no moral rule applies to that sphere of activity other than the principles that govern every aspect of life: honesty, courage, common humanity, consideration. As in all else, what counts in sex life is that it is wrong to harm others. This is the only sexual morality that exists: you shall not use your sex to gain power or influence over others; you shall not injure them, and you shall not cause them unnecessary pain.

"Whatever else you do, so long as you do not harm anyone, concerns no one but yourself and the person you are with. To abstain from sexual pleasure is no more virtuous than to abstain from picking flowers, from reading books, or from going skiing.

"If you can really derive joy and pleasure from your sex, then that is of great moral value, because we live in difficult times, where the greatest sin is to abandon hope—and the greatest crime is to lose the courage to live. All joys and pleasures—*which don't harm others*—but which can serve to strengthen the enjoyment of living and the courage to live, are to the good, including sexual pleasures.

"I'll repeat what I said a minute ago—most people ruin their own and other people's sex lives by thinking only of themselves. One thinks only of one's own desire, one's own joy, one's own orgasm. When you get to the point where you can think more about the other person's orgasm than about your own, then you're grown up—and the remarkable thing is that only then can you yourself really get full pleasure out of the whole thing. When you no longer lie there just waiting for it to happen to you, that's when it really starts happening.

"You know yourself what you were doing with Henry. It was wrong, don't you think?"

"Yes," I nodded.

"The cause of your doing it," he went on, "is not anything about yourself, but the egotistical and untrue so-called sexual morality that you had ground into you by your mother and grandmother. You were embarrassed and ashamed and had a guilty conscience over your sexual instincts and so on—and instead of telling him what you'd like to have him do to you, you took revenge on him.

"Next time you meet someone like Henry, you must be able to instruct him, make a decent lover out of him. But in order to do that, three things are needed: first, you must think only of *him;* second, you mustn't be embarrassed; third, you must know how to do something yourself.

"Let me put it another way. Most women are so inhibited by shame and guilt feelings that they've forgotten how to take an active part themselves. They lie down like a log and let the man take it from there.

"What you need now is to learn to be active, to learn to think more of him than of yourself. Do you understand?"

"Yes," I said. I was trembling a bit inside. I had been looking forward to enjoying myself in his arms. Instead it had turned out to be a new step in the treatment.

He walked over and lay down on the table.

"Go ahead," he said, "now it's your turn to be active. But gently, gently. When you meet a new Henry, don't scare him to death."

So it was my turn. Right away I noticed that I was embarrassed. Actually, not embarrassed sexually, but in a different way. I waited a moment.

"Now, if you can find out what *I* like," he said, "and make sure that I get the most possible pleasure out of it, that's all there is to it."

His organ hadn't yet come up again, so I leaned over and rubbed my breasts against his chest. Then I did the same with him as with Brita—I licked him on the nipples, and strangely enough they reacted in the same way as with a woman: they got bigger and stiffer. I had never suspected that this happened with men too, and I asked if he liked it. That wasn't necessary, because the answer was quite apparent.

I licked him on the navel and farther down on his stomach, and I began to enjoy it. I was learning things the whole time I was examining him. But the essence of it was that he reacted in the same way and to the same things that I did. That made me

feel more secure, even though it was new to be playing an active role myself. Not that it was unnatural,
just a little unusual to begin with.

I concentrated next on his pecker, which was now
good and stiff and still shiny from the oil I had used
on him. I felt like playing with it for a long time, and
I took careful hold of the tip with the fingers of one
hand, so he'd be sure to feel my nails. Out at the
very point was a shiny drop, and with the tip of one
finger I spread this drop out over the head of his
organ. You can be sure he wasn't lying altogether
still as I was doing this. It's a strange fluid, even
slicker than oil. I pulled the skin slowly back and
forth, then tickled him around the rim under the
head, which made him give a couple of mighty
twitches with his legs. My fingers slid down his
pecker, down the thick shaft to the root, where the
wreath of hair was—just like the grass that grows
around a tree. It struck me that this strong organ was
much more plant than animal, a sort of prehistoric
plant with a big, hard flower on top with a slit where
the fertile pollen could shoot out. But what a sensitive
plant it was.

I pulled the skin way down, to see as much as I
could, and at the same time my fingers went up
under his testicles, which were quite a bit bigger
than Henry's. Scratching at them carefully, I put my
mouth down to his organ and kissed it. He writhed,
and I kept on kissing him over the whole thing,
especially on the head where the feeling is strongest
—hard, wet kisses for a while, then gentle, cautious
ones. I stuck my tongue way out and used just the
point to lick him. His pecker stiffened into iron. It

was sticky all over from my saliva and from the liquid that was coming from the tip. I took the end of it in my mouth, for the first time doing something I'd always yearned to do but had never dared before. I think I enjoyed it as much as he did. My mouth felt as if it were located between my legs. Down below, of course, I was wet myself.

I kept it in my mouth, licking the head. Now and then I would suck on it, then bite carefully at the throat just below the head. He was squirming, and I knew that I had to be careful to keep him from coming too soon. It just had to last, it was so lovely for both of us. I took it out of my mouth and began to lick at his testicles, then kissed him underneath and around them, noticing that if I took hold of the sack above the balls, and squeezed it hard, but not too hard, it had a really strong effect on him. His organ throbbed and seemed to get even stiffer.

I crept up on the table and sat down on his stomach. I smiled at him, and he smiled back.

I moved farther down and felt his pecker against my backside. It stood up straight now, and I got up over him on all fours, so that my breasts hung down against his face. I bent forward a little, and sure enough—he couldn't help biting at them. He took them in his lips and sucked, and I felt more and more like having that red pole stuck into me.

I waited a bit, then backed up again until I could feel the head of his organ right between my buttocks. A bit more, and I could feel it in the middle of my crotch. I helped things along with my hand, and when I could feel it at the right place, I lowered my abdomen so that it stuck into me a bit. My God, it felt good after all these preliminaries I'd been initiating.

He tossed back and forth underneath me, shut his eyes, clenched his teeth together, and turned his head from side to side. I sank farther down and it slipped into me. My flower stretched out, took it in, and closed tightly around him. We seemed to be stuck together, and I started moving slowly up and down, up and down. I lowered my head to look between my arms, past my breasts, to where our hairs joined. I got a good view of the whole process. When I sank down, it disappeared into me, and when I raised up it came back into view. Then I started getting very cautious, doing it so carefully that only the very head of his pecker was in me. I moved hardly at all, but I itched in the abdomen like one possessed. Suddenly I lost all control—I sat down all the way on him and got going at full speed. He grabbed me around the arms and pulled me to him with a terrific groan. He came, filling me with his warm juice.

I felt wet and wonderful in my groin, but horribly horny and unsatisfied, since I hadn't come at the same time. And yet I was not displeased or unhappy; it was easy for me to have an orgasm with him, and I knew that this had been a new experiment and that I had learned something to make me healthier and more active. If it had lasted just an instant longer, I would have had an orgasm too.

At the same time, I was glad that he had enjoyed it, both because it was someone I liked so much and because I was pleased and proud to have handled a man so well that he lay there as happy and satisfied as a little baby—without having made the least effort himself.

I was pleased, and I got on top of him to cuddle with him.

Actually, I just wanted to lie in his arms the usual way, mouth to mouth and breast to breast, just lying there whether he got it up again or not, just lying there—preferably, of course, noticing it grow and get back into fighting trim again and then just lie on my back quite normally, lift up my knees, and let him in between my legs from above so that I could feel his whole weight. But it was good lying there with him anyway, even if that plant of his was little and soft.

"Yes," he said, suddenly awake, but with his arms still around me, "this is a typical situation, which you'll go through often, where the man comes before you've had an orgasm yourself. Either the two of you may for various reasons be unable to go on— and in that case you must never show that you are disappointed over not coming—or you may have the time and opportunity to go on, and then it's up to you to make him potent and put him back in shape while you yourself are still on the verge. So you've got to get him going as quickly as possible, and the second time around he'll take more time to reach a climax. That's *your* big chance. What do you do to a man to get him ready for action in a hurry? If his desire is lacking, so is his ability. What do you do with him to arouse his desire and with it his ability? There he is, in the condition the French call *la petite mort,* and what are you going to do about it? Do you know?"

"I think I do," I said and smiled.

I felt lightheaded and confused, and it hurt to tear myself out of his arms. But I went into the bathroom, got a towel, a bar of soap, and a bowl of warm water, and back I was again. He smiled when he saw what I had brought.

"Actually, you do know a little already," he said. "You're quick to learn."

"Shhh!" I said. "Lie still."

I began by washing him around his organ. Next I put my wet hand around the plant itself and soaped up his soft thing and his testicles until suds began to form.

"Well," I said, "how's it going?"

"Thank you," he said. "It's beginning to be rather nice. Just keep it up!"

I went on, affectionately and solicitously, and it wasn't long before the first signs of life appeared. It got longer and bigger and a bit firmer in my hand. I dried it carefully with the towel, and gave it a going-over with oil from the tip on back, and then once again in the opposite direction. It was growing all the time, but it was still not firm enough to be of any use. I slowly rubbed the oil off it, and then licked around the rim under the head. It assumed its full strength and dignity again. I felt proud of my work, which actually hadn't taken very long. I kept up with the licking and sucking, mouthed it, and bit around the trunk and at the root. I had lain on top of him, but in the opposite direction, with my backside toward him, and now I could feel his fingers in my slit. They were swift and sure, and I noticed that the muscles in my back were twitching. So I spread my legs across him, one on each side of his head, still holding his organ in my mouth. He kissed me along my legs, then put his mouth against my flower. A moment later his tongue came into me and began to lick my clitoris. I kept his sex in my mouth, and it was wonderful to have this contact in two places at the same time. We worked each other into convulsions, until he broke things off. By this time I could only think of one thing: to get under him and let him kiss me on the mouth while we did it in the way I was used to and liked best of all. But no!

"I'll show you something," he said. "Sit on top of me like last time, all the way down."

I didn't show my disappointment, because it was his turn to arrange things, and in a jiffy I was sitting up there, riding on his hips, impaled as nicely as could be. He put his hand down into my flower, and his finger found my clitoris right away. Spears shot through me again, and I smiled, knowing what it was he wanted to show me—the advantage that this position really offered: letting the man get at the right place easily with his hand if the woman had difficulty coming. That wasn't my problem now, and if he hadn't stopped I would have had an orgasm right up there in the saddle.

"Turn around," he ordered. "Sit the same way you are now, but with your back toward me."

I did as he said, feeling a little strange.

"Lie down in front," he said gently, "and stretch your legs out and back toward me."

I followed his instructions and found myself once more in the turned-around position, but now with my face between his feet and my rear toward his face. Because my legs were spread, he had a superb view of what was going to happen. But he improved his insight still more by pulling my buttocks apart, making absolutely everything visible. That plant of his was inside me, stiff as a board and resisting to the utmost a position that tended to bend it in the middle. It was a glorious feeling, but it tensed me up inside.

"Now you can start moving," he said softly.

I raised my hips and lowered them again a couple of times. It was a real shock to feel how hard his pecker strained against the front of my slit with each movement. My clitoris was getting a massage that was about all I could stand, and I may have done a bit of shrieking. I kept on going and could feel my insides getting ready to come; my muscles were contracting and working by themselves. Then with a quick motion he twisted away and out of me.

"No," I cried. "No!"

He laughed, and in spite of the painfulness of the interruption I had to laugh myself. He turned over on his side and laughed, reaching his arms out to me. I crept up to him and lay with my breasts against his chest, and he kissed me and stroked my hair until I rolled over on my back and everything disappeared in a sea of warm waves under him.

This final part of Dr. Peterson's treatment was dedicated to making me as versatile, as active, and as unselfish as possible. A few weeks remained, and by the time I had graduated from school, I think Dr.

Peterson's therapy had borne very fine fruit. It was just too bad for Henry that he wouldn't have anything more to do with me.

That summer I took my first trip abroad, and Dr. Peterson and I had a pleasant farewell. It was the third time we drank champagne together, and I received an especially fine treatment from him—this time as a girl friend rather than as a patient, to the great delight of us both.

When I said good-bye to him, Dr. Peterson told me, "Remember the most important moral principle of all: Do unto others as you would have others do unto you. It applies to the field of love as to all others."

And so I went my way, out into the wide world. Beyond a doubt, Dr. Peterson had prepared me wisely and thoroughly for almost anything I might encounter out there.

He had lit a fire in me that was going to be hard to put out.

It was the fire of benevolence, compassion, and charity. Of all things on this earth there's nothing like the unity of spiritual and physical love, Eros and Agape in union, the true *caritas,* love in body and in soul.

Just think what that could mean for the cause of democracy!

I had my work cut out for me.

4

I headed happily away along Route 1. South, toward the Mediterranean.

My parents had been against this trip, but there wasn't much they could say, the way they themselves had behaved—my father with his girls and mother with all her lovers from times past. There'd been little enough of that for her in the past few years, and she'd concentrated on grumbling instead. No, they didn't have much to offer when it came to upholding moral principles.

Don't misunderstand me. I have nothing against my parents on that account. Absolutely nothing. Why shouldn't they be allowed to act like other men and women? What I don't like is the way they try to act as if they've always been so irreproachably noble— or, to put it better, I don't like the meaning they give to the word "noble." What's more, I don't care for scenes. I don't like sulking. I don't like grumbling. As far as I'm concerned, my parents can have their sexual urges when they allow me the same thing.

It was, of course, tough getting my way with this hiking trip through Europe. But I had graduated with honors, and there was no way to find fault with me. I got what I wanted.

I walked along the side of the road. Under the soles of my feet was the highway to the Continent. The world lay before me—even if I did have to get through Sweden and Denmark first. I was marching south, I really was!

In blue jeans, shirt, and sweater, with a knapsack on my back.

In time with my steps, I sang a song I remembered by heart from my schooldays—one of those stupid songs from grammar school, but it was good music to march to. "Brave in heart, sharp in mind, strong in arm and leg. That's the kind of boys our country needs!" But I sang different words to it, which I'd made up myself:

> Up with skirts,
> Down with pants,
> Out with arms and legs.
> That's the kind of girls our country needs!

I had made up the words one evening at a dance, and it was a big hit, even if it wasn't exactly anything to compare with the poetry of Ibsen.

I tramped vigorously on, with car after car roaring past me heading south, really south!

The next car I tried to stop.

Zoom! It disappeared past me like a flash.

The next car too. Whoosh! Gone.

A few more cars went by in the same fashion. No one saw me or took notice of me.

Then along came a Volkswagen bus.

I struck as fine a pose as possible by the side of the road, and I'd hardly put out my hand before it screeched to a halt.

I noticed that it had a Swedish license plate. On the panel was a trade mark and in large letters:

VITALIAFILM INC.. I knew that the Swedes were a cinematic people, so it didn't surprise me. A man in his thirties sat at the wheel.

He gave me a friendly smile. "Come on," he said, "hop in."

I curtsied sweetly and thanked him. I handed my knapsack to him, he put it in the back of the bus, and I got in and sat down next to him. In the back I saw some technical equipment—cables, a couple of movie cameras, floodlights.

He told me that he'd been shooting cultural scenes in Norway: folk-dancing, bird life, and trout fishers.

He was pleasant and looked fine. Medium blond and a bit plump.

As time went by, he told about all there was to tell about himself: divorce, unhappy childhood, a fairly difficult manhood. When I say "manhood," I don't mean that he had difficulty with any male organ, but simply with the years of his manhood. His main interests were dance music, sports, and movies. He wasn't exactly what you'd call unique, but he was nice.

If he'd told me what kind of movies he liked best, he'd have aroused more interest in me. But all he said was that he was going to shoot a couple of scenes in Göteborg the next day and then travel to Stockholm.

It turned out he had a bottle of rum in his glove compartment. Life brightened up for us both as I sat next to him with a big jar in my hand, mixing rum and orange juice in it. He even had ice cubes in a container.

We crossed the border into Sweden and drove on through a few small towns and country villages. Once in a while we could see the sea as we talked, smoked, and drank together. He didn't so much as put his hand on my knee, and I began to get suspicious.

I was a little disappointed too, because I liked him a lot and would have enjoyed going out with him that evening in Göteborg. I wondered whether there was something wrong with my appearance or something wrong with him.

He may have sensed what I was thinking, because just then he did put his hand on my knee, and since I didn't exactly scream with fright about a fate worse than death, he went right on up my tight blue jeans and felt my crotch from the outside.

"Skaal!" I said, raising my glass.

He must have known the way from before, because just a minute or two later he turned off the highway into a narrow road that ran through a forest. He found a still narrower road, and a bit later he stopped the bus.

Most of this time he'd kept his hand on my jeans, so I was in the right mood by the time we arrived.

The driver's seat was uncomfortable and didn't lend itself to what we had in mind, so we jumped out and hopped into the back of the bus. There wasn't much room to lie down in there either.

We both took off our pants, and I saw that his stalk had risen up in full splendor. We sat and smoked, while he held his hand inside my panties, which were getting wetter all the time. Then he went cautiously to work inside the edges of the slit. I straightened my back and twisted myself into a more accessible position, so I was sitting on the floor of the truck with my back to some cables and my knees up. He stuck a finger way in and pulled it out again. Then he kneeled down and tucked his shirttail high up around his waist.

"Turn around," he said. I didn't get what he meant.

"Turn your back to me and get down on all fours," he explained. "There's so damn little room in here."

Now I got what he was driving at. I stood halfway up, because of the roof of the bus, and pulled my panties down to my ankles so I could move my knees better. I turned my back to him and kneeled on the floor in front of him, pulling my shirt way up, just as he had done. As he kneeled behind me, I leaned back a bit, and felt his hard pecker against my backside. I wagged my bottom against it, then leaned forward and put my hands on the floor. I waited on all fours with my rear toward him, then felt him separate my buttocks, hunting for the right spot. He found it all right, and I gave a little yelp when he stuck it into me. First just a bit, and then farther in. I wasn't lying completely still, but pushing myself against him and moving my rear to one side and then the other. He held me under the stomach with one hand and rubbed the small of my back with the other, while his stomach brushed my bottom. He did it slowly and then fast, and when I reached my hand back between my legs, I could feel his balls swinging like a pendulum. I wrapped my hand around them and tickled my way up to where his shaft began. Then I touched his pecker itself as it was going in and out of my body, so stiff, thick, and wet. I carefully let him feel my fingernails on his plant and on the head of it. Suddenly he let go his grip under my stomach and took tight hold of my hips. A couple more in-and-outs and he pressed all the way down on me and poured it into me. He rested on my back for a moment like a damp rag, then said, "My God! Oh my God!"

He sat down on the floor.

I lit a cigarette and gave it to him, then took the mug and filled it with our favorite drink, one part rum and two parts orange juice. He leaned back and smiled, while his organ hung its head. I wasn't going to let it get away with that, and when he'd had a swallow or two of our drink and a puff on the cigarette, I put my fingers under his balls as if I wanted to play a bit. I scratched gently underneath them, and also tickled him under his plant, now completely soft.

He started laughing.

I stretched my legs out on the floor and put my head in his lap so that I had his organ right in front of my face. Very carefully I touched it with the tip of my tongue, and I felt a shudder go through him. I brushed my mouth against it a few times and could tell that it was about ready to come back to life. I licked him hard around the root, and then over and under all the way out to the underside of the head. It started growing noticeably now, and when I took it deep in my mouth it was fairly stiff again. It was big and somewhat different from Dr. Peterson's. The head was smaller, but the trunk itself was thicker. The length was about the same. I sucked at it contentedly and gave him a chance to drink a bit and smoke some more of his cigarette. Then I started biting at the purple head and at the trunk. He opened the front of my shirt and massaged my breasts, while his organ kept getting harder and harder. When he pushed me down on the floor again, I resumed the same position, with my backside toward him and my hands on the floor.

"Bend down," he said, "so your head's on the floor. Rest it on your hands."

I did as he said and felt my damp hindquarters spread open to him. He didn't waste any time in pulling my buttocks apart and pushing himself into me. At the same time, he began to rub me around the other opening with one of his fingers, and a little later he put his finger right in. It felt so good I groaned and bit my knuckles. I actually shrieked as I felt my backside, my abdomen, and everything else starting to melt. Those enormous muscular spasms came at definite, regular intervals, and I tried to hold my hands around my head and keep my legs still. I came in two long surges, quite close together, and when he shot the juice of life up into me for the second time, we were coming together.

A while later I sat beside him in the front seat, dressed and made up again. We were back on the highway. We both felt warm and satisfied, good all over.

"You're not so terribly shy," he said.

"No," I said, "not any more."

"If you want," he continued, "you can earn some real money tomorrow."

"How?"

He smiled. "We're filming a couple of scenes in the morning."

"You mean you want to take movies of me?"

"That's right," he said, "if you can be just as unshy as today."

"Are you crazy?" was all I said.

"You'll be paid two thousand crowns."

"Swedish?"

"Of course."

I did some figuring. It really was a lot of money, and it would mean a world of difference to my travel funds. It was tempting, and I thought it over. The movies would, of course, be secret, but . . . it wasn't much fun to be exhibited in the altogether to people who might happen to know me.

"O.K.," he said, "three thousand."

That wasn't exactly a bad offer for half a day's work.

"Will my face be visible?"

"Not really. And you'll be heavily made up beforehand."

"What do I do?"

"The same as this morning. Plus a bit more. Nothing that hurts, no whipping or anything like that."

"Three thousand Swedish crowns?"

"Right. But that's tops. You're not the only girl."

"Who do I do it with?"

"A fellow who's a little older than you. Real good-looking."

I sat there thinking about it. Three thousand Swedish crowns meant that I could travel for a longer time and much more comfortably than I had planned. The whole trip would be something different. I'd have more time to look at old churches and museums, to broaden and develop myself . . . and I do like good food.

"Well?" he said.

"O.K.," I answered, "tomorrow."

He drove on for a while in silence, then said, "I'll drive you to your hotel in Göteborg, and you stay in your room this evening. Take a bath and go to bed early. Sleep well. We want you in good shape tomorrow morning. Wide awake and in fine fettle. Is that clear?"

"Yes," I answered. "Is he a handsome fellow?"

"Very handsome and very strong, and with an endurance you just won't believe. We've used him a couple of times before. His name is Mikkel, and he's a gypsy."

"A *gypsy?*"

"Yes, but he isn't violent. He plays the violin."

"Violin? Is he good at it?"

"He'll bring his violin case along, so you'll have a chance to hear him."

"When'll that be?"

"Nine-thirty tomorrow morning. You'll be picked up at the hotel, and your bill will be paid."

When we got to Göteborg, he drove me to a women's hotel, where I found a room. His name was Göran, and as he drove away I saw once again the name on the side of the bus: VITALIAFILM INC.

Of course, I really felt like going out right away and having a look at the town, but a promise is a promise, and I kept to my room. I took a bath, washed myself thoroughly all over and lay down in bed with a book, Bjørnson's *Fishing Girl*. I turned off the light at about ten, feeling pleased with my first day on the road.

I lay in the dark, thinking things over. The trip had started off well and seemed promising. With my travel funds increased by three thousand Swedish crowns, things had changed for the better.

It was, after all, Dr. Peterson I had to thank for everything, and I thought about how much I owed him. I also thought how good it would be to have him here in bed, just to lie in his arms and be happy, or else to do whatever he might feel like.

I think I dreamt about him that night.

5

I awoke, cheerful and rested, before eight. I did my exercises, took a shower, and had breakfast in my room. Bad coffee and sweet Swedish bread. But the milk, the grapefruit juice, and the Danish pastry tasted good.

The phone rang. It was the front desk.

Göran had come to pick me up. I slung my knapsack, already packed, over my shoulder and walked downstairs to meet him, well-rested, happy, and all set to go to work.

He had a different vehicle this time, a regular passenger car with no name on it. We drove over to another part of town, parked the car, and walked in through a long entryway, across a courtyard, and finally up a steep flight of stairs. At the top was a door with a sign on it, "Anderson Photography" or something similar. We went into a large, old-fashioned photographic studio.

A tall, rather heavy-set man in his forties was standing there. He seemed pleasant enough, and he smiled.

"Hello," said Göran, "this is Bengt, our make-up man. And this is Lillian. Doesn't she look fine?"

We shook hands, and he bowed.

"She does look fine. We'll manage all right."

"Is Mikkel here?" Göran asked.

"No," said Bengt. "Mikkel called in. He's held up. But we can take the boys first."

Then I saw that farther back in the studio two boys were sitting, one of them quite young, probably about sixteen or seventeen, and the other a bit older. Both were wearing dressing gowns with nothing underneath. A slight shudder went through me as I realized how heavily both were made up.

"Is Mikkel coming for sure?" said Göran.

"Yes," answered Bengt, "he needs money these days."

"O.K., boys!" shouted Göran. "Let's get going."

I stood there a little bewildered, while the two boys took off their robes. What should I do? Stay here and wait?

"You can stick around and watch," said Bengt in a fatherly way. "It won't hurt you any."

"Yes," said Göran, "of course."

The two boys, completely naked now, walked over to the middle of the floor, where there was a bed, made up but without blankets. They giggled at each other and seemed to have real zest for their work.

"Heini!" shouted Göran, "all set!"

Heini loomed forth from the background. He was a workman in his twenties, with a dark beard and a cigarette in his mouth. He put it out and stood waiting for orders. He was obviously the technician who was going to handle the lighting. In any event, that's what he did. The boys sat down on the edge of the bed. The younger one already had an erection like a full-grown man's, in fact about like Henry's from the old days, but with very little hair around his pecker. Both boys were made up over their entire bodies and wore rouge and lipstick on their faces. Then the camera was turned on.

The smaller one, who had the erection, lay back, and the other bent over him and stroked his chest. He, too, began to grow erect, and he lay down so that both peckers came into contact. It was fun to watch, and as the light changed and the camera hummed away I saw a few things that were new to me. The boys lay on their backs, side by side, kissing each other on the mouth, while their plants waved in the air, and then the older one took the other's organ in his hand and pushed the skin back and forth. The smaller one had skin covering the head of his, like Henry, even when it was stiff and upright.

Just then Göran called out, "Cut!"

The boys lay still again, and then the younger one took hold of the other's organ and fondled it. I looked at the boys' faces, and both were smiling blissfully. They rubbed their peckers together, slowly and carefully, until the next halt.

Now the older one put his head down in the small one's lap and began licking him carefully on his little testicles and then along the shaft and out to the tip. The sixteen-year-old strained joyfully, while the other kept at his work slowly and thoroughly.

"Cut!" cried Göran. "All right, action!"

Now they changed roles, and it was the older one who lay on his back with his sex pointing straight up, and the small one who used his mouth and tongue. He put it all the way in his mouth, and the boy who was lying down raised his stomach so that his back formed an arc over the bed. He gasped while the other kept on licking and sucking. They changed roles again, and with the camera much closer up the younger one lay down on his back and spread his legs as far apart as he could. The other inserted a finger up his backside and continued sucking, but just out at the very tip and very carefully. The way the small one was thrashing around, it was obvious that cream was going to flow in a few seconds.

I felt awfully funny standing there watching, and I could feel that down inside my panties my own slick juice was starting to flow. I felt like lying down with the boys, young as they were.

"Cut!" roared Göran.

Next it was the big one who lay down, and the small one placed a finger between his buttocks and worked it in. I'll never forget the look on the face of the older one when that happened, for the young one had also mouthed his organ at the same time. It was almost more exciting to watch his face than what was going on between his legs.

After a while the small one lay down on his back, while the big one got on top of him, as on a girl. The small one opened his legs, and the other stuck his pecker between them. Then the little one shut his legs together, and the other started moving up and down. The young one, lying underneath, responded just the way I myself—and I suppose most girls—do. He twisted like a snake, shut his eyes and bit his tongue, while the other kept at it between his legs. You could tell the younger boy was enjoying it.

"Cut!" said Göran. "Now for the final scene. Turn around, my boy!"

The small one got up. He was flushed in the face and a bit sweaty, but his pride and joy stood out straight as a stick.

"It hurts," said the boy. "A little, anyway."

"Turn around," said the older one. "It won't take long."

The little one looked at his friend, put his arms around his neck, and kissed him on the mouth.

"All right," he said, "whatever you say."

He turned over on his stomach and lay with his round, white bottom up in the air and his legs partly spread. He put his face down on the sheet, holding his head in his hands. and then raised his rear up a bit more toward his friend, who had kneeled down between his legs and was rubbing oil into the small one's opening. Next, with the camera still turning, the big one pushed his pecker into the young one's rear, slowly and cautiously but forcefully. The boy writhed underneath him, and you could see that he liked it even if it hurt. He lay down flat on his stomach, and his friend pushed his shaft deep into him. Both were groaning and shouting now.

The big fellow came mightily, and as soon as he was finished he turned the small one over on his back, so his glistening, rigid pecker came into sight. He took it in his mouth, all the way, and the small one yelped, twisting his hips back and forth with the spasms that were now beginning. Just as his convulsions really got going, the other took it out of his mouth, worked at it a while with his hand, and then caught the whole load right in his face.

"Cut!" said Göran. "Good work!"

The boys' scene was over, and I hadn't even noticed that someone new had come into the room. He was an unusually attractive guest, with black hair and the whitest teeth I have ever seen on a human being. He had a violin case under his arm.

Mikkel was here.

The boys disappeared into one of the dressing rooms. They came out after a while and talked with Göran, who wrote out a check. They shook hands politely with each of us, and left.

"Let's go," said Bengt, "the dressing room's empty now, and I'll wait for you in the make-up room."

Mikkel had already undressed in the studio and put his clothes neatly over a chair. He was wonderful to behold, with narrow hips and smooth, powerful muscles. The growth of hair under his stomach, between his nipples, and on his head was as black as a crow. It was curly with a bluish shine to it.

He seemed so free and easy, standing there naked among the rest of us.

While Mikkel went into the make-up room with Bengt, I went to the dressing room, where there was fortunately a shower too. When I had undressed, I went to the make-up room, where Bengt was still working on Mikkel—over his whole body, just like the two boys.

Mikkel was lying back in a sort of large dentist's chair, and when he saw me in the nude his pecker rose up on the spot.

I felt honored that he had raised the flag for me so quickly, and while his pecker was erect Bengt started making it up too. Everyone, on his face, his chest, his stomach, his sex, and his groin, he was using colors that one never sees in real life. The whole business looked so strange and unreal, except for Mikkel's black eyes and that magnificent, powerful organ of his. It was thickest out at the tip, and it rose like an oak tree from his growth of hair, with a lovely crown on top of it.

"There you are," said Bengt, "all set."

Mikkel got up, and I sat down in the chair, which automatically tilted back, so that I was flat on my back.

"This may surprise you a bit," said Bengt, "but it has to be."

Right away I felt his rubbing my whole flower with warm soapsuds. Mikkel laughed, and I smiled at him. With a soft brush, Bengt soaped me for a good while. It didn't hurt, and Mikkel stood there watching. Then Bengt scooped the suds off me with one sweep of his left hand. As carefully as could be, he began shaving my flower. It felt good.

When he was finished, I looked just like a little girl, but a bit different in size.

Next came the make-up over my whole body— rouge, powder, and lipstick on my face, and body make-up everywhere else. Bengt's soft fingers slid even between my buttocks to my most secret opening. I had to lie face down when he did that, but I turned my head to the side so I could see Mikkel, who was keeping close track of the whole operation. We smiled at each other.

Finally we were both ready.

Back in the studio Göran and Heini were hard at work. They'd put clean sheets on the bed, which looked fresh and smooth now. I liked cleanliness like that. I appreciate such things.

While they were arranging the lights, I took a look at myself in the mirror. I was still the same person, but what I saw was a different edition of myself, with much darker skin and all my contours more strongly accentuated. Between my buttocks I was made up lighter than natural, everywhere else darker.

"Why do I need so much make-up?" I asked Bengt.

"Movies are the opposite of nature," he said. "If you're going to look natural on film, I have to make you completely unnatural before we begin."

"Have you been in the movie business a long time?" I asked.

"All my life," he said. "I've been making those so-called art films, which after all deal with the same thing as here. I'm fed up with that shit. This stuff here is healthier and more honest. And there's not all that much risk in it."

"Could you go to jail for it?" I asked.

"For a long time," Bengt said. I could still feel the effect of his sensitive fingers over my whole body. I liked Bengt.

"We don't sell them here in Sweden at all," he went on. "We develop them, destroy the originals, and send them abroad on microfilm, mostly to England and the United States. But we don't let them be shown for a year's time—that way it's impossible to trace them. We have a lot of NATO people for customers. A lot of them go to Germany, too, also Italy."

Göran interrupted us. "On stage!"

I lay down on the bed with Mikkel. He put his arms around me right away and laughed. Then he took one of my nipples between those white teeth of his.

"Cut!" cried Göran. "What the hell do you think this is? A marriage clinic or something?"

We all laughed.

"We do things properly here," he went on. "This isn't going to be screwing for the fun of it. It's going to be hard, honest work. I'm going to direct every move you make, but I want to make one thing clear from the start: Lillian, do exactly what you're told, and yet don't let Mikkel come. You've got to stop every time he gets close to an orgasm. Is that clear? Can you manage it?"

What a job!

"I'll do my best," I said shyly.

Our day's work began, step by step as Göran had said, and interrupted constantly by him and Heini because of technical problems. I'll just tell what we did to each other, since these technical details soon get tiresome.

For a while we lay face to face and kissed each other on the mouth. He made good use of his tongue, under my lips and tongue, and licked on the outer part of my lips; then his strong tongue pushed through between my lips, just as if it had been working its way into my slit itself. I could feel his pecker hard against my stomach, and it was damp at the tip. One of my hands slipped down by itself, felt around his shaft, and took one of the thick, shiny drops up to my mouth. He began licking me in the ears and on the neck, without touching me down below, and when he was through with that, he licked me from my neck to the soles of my feet. He lay me face down and licked my back, pulled my buttocks apart and let his tongue slide along the whole crack. The small spot between the openings got thoroughly licked, and he licked the back opening until I didn't know my own name. Then he turned me over on my back and put his tongue deep into my slit and moved it, not in and out but back and forth. He licked my clitoris until it stood way out, then took it between his lips, then in his mouth, letting it slip slowly out and sucking it back in again.

He lay down on his back, and I sat bottom first in his face, rubbing my flower against his mouth while he bit and sucked and licked. I leaned forward and bit at his organ, put his testicles in my mouth one after the other, and licked him all over his pecker, finally taking it almost down my throat and letting it slide out again. I kissed it around the head and at the neck.

Now I lay on my back, and he put his knees one on each side of my head, bending down far enough so that I could reach his testicles and his shaft with my mouth.

I stuck my right index finger down in my crotch, getting it good and slippery. Then I inserted it between his buttocks, into that tight, warm opening, while he twisted and turned and almost collapsed on me. Finally he did lie down on me and put his face between my legs again. We licked and sucked at each other that way until Göran cut it off.

Next I lay down on my back with my legs over Mikkel's shoulders, one knee over each shoulder, while he stuck his pecker in, all the way to rock bottom. He did that just a couple of times, then held it still, just barely in me. Still as could be, while he looked me in the eye and laughed.

All this was filmed as a close-up from the rear, so you could see the organs slipping in and out of each other. In addition, Mikkel held position while Göran took a couple of stills of the situation.

I was right at the brink of an orgasm now, but I wasn't allowed to move, and it hurt terribly over my whole body. I sat on top of Mikkel for a while, still without moving, but with him inside me. I straddled him in both directions, frontward and backward. When I lay down frontward, with my face between his feet, in order to feel the tightness of his pecker inside me, he jammed a finger into my tightest opening. It wasn't slick or oily, and it hurt just beautifully there. At the same time, his pecker was pressing hard against my clitoris. That was all it took. I let out a scream and twisted my whole abdomen against his, while the warm stream gave away inside me, gushing and gushing. I thought I was ready to go crazy, and I had no idea what anyone else was doing.

When I came to again, Mikkel was still lying there, oak tree and all.

I started licking him under the testicles, by the roots of the plant, where you can feel the stalk that goes on forever.

He was still quite calm and put his hands in my hair as I worked on.

Coming as powerfully as I had didn't seem to have the effect of quieting me down. That pretty, warm, brown body of Mikkel's put me right back in shape in no time.

I had to lie face down, with my legs apart, but with my abdomen flat against the bed. When Mikkel opened me up from behind and pushed his pecker into the front opening, I couldn't keep still, but rose to my knees, while he followed right along until he was on his knees too. Then he went slowly on—all the way in, all the way out. Slower and slower. Finally he held it just barely in, maybe a quarter of an inch or so. I was dying, and I knew it was just as bad for him. His body trembled, and he was breathing heavily and groaning. Every muscle in his body was tensed, and the same was true with me. All we'd have had to do was make one or two moves, and we'd have both been off in a whirl. But we kept still because Göran was watching us like a hawk. Our facial expressions were being filmed now, and the two of us must have been a sight to see.

Then Göran interrupted, "Cut!"

He obviously had us both where he wanted us now. We were both on the verge of a climax, right on the brink of exploding.

"Bend your head all the way down," he said to me, "and pull your buttocks wide apart."

I did as he said and had the feeling that it would be impossible to be more exposed than I was—with my tail in the air and everything wide open. My groin and abdomen were on fire, and I could have screamed. Almost without noticing it I pushed my rear toward Mikkel, getting his pecker a little farther in me. Not more than a quarter of an inch, I think. Mikkel shook and moaned.

"No!" screamed Göran. "Hold it there! And look this way!"

Helplessly chained to each other, we looked at the camera.

"Now for a new position," said Göran. "Kneel down on the floor with the upper part of your body on the bed."

I did as he said, and Mikkel came along with me. It was just as bad as before, and I twisted and fretted. Mikkel tried to move his pecker a little, but Göran stopped him.

Next I lay on my back on the bed, with my knees over the bottom edge and my feet on the floor. Mikkel put it in from the front, and I could feel the juice run out of me. We were interrupted once again. I lay down on my back in bed with my knees up and with Mikkel lying crosswise under my knees. He got in from below, and at the same time put his fingers on my clitoris. I yelped. Then we were stopped. I could feel in the roots of my hair and at the tips of my fingers that if I didn't come soon I'd go crazy. But every time Mikkel's enormous, thick plant had slipped in and out of me a couple of times, Göran would order a new position.

"Face to face! Lie there the normal way. And get to work!"

When I felt his pecker pushing into me once more, and this time from the front, I bit him in the face. I licked him, kissed him and bit him, and the muscles in his brown body tightened until the whole man was a hard, heavy rock. He got bigger inside me, and I cried along with him, tossing my head back and forth and scratching him on the shoulders and across his back. He held one hand under my seat and one hand around my shoulders, clutching at me as though he wanted to squeeze the juice right out of me. And that's exactly what he did. We were just one tangled-up mass, and the whole world started spinning around. I don't remember it too clearly, and by this time I must have been partly unconscious. In any case

I came just as his juice shot into me, and I came with every inch of my body, back and front, top and bottom, in my neck and stomach, all at the same time.

Afterward I was just dead. But Mikkel sat calmly on the edge of the bed and smoked. Brown and black and pretty with those perfect white teeth like a beast of prey.

I couldn't even manage a smile.

Bengt came over quietly and gave me a cigarette. "Good for you," he said gently. "You're doing fine."

"Shall we get back to work?" said Mikkel.

I looked at him and couldn't believe my own eyes: that plant of his, which I thought was hanging soft and loose between his legs, was waving cheerfully up in the air like a flagpole.

I felt tender down below, sweaty and quite weak.

"Let her have a drink," said Göran, "and we'll see."

"No," I said, "I'd love something to drink, but I just can't do it any more now."

The gypsy boy looked at me and smiled again.

"I've heard that before," he said. "I can wear out two or three women in a row."

He lay down on his back, with his head against my hip, and laughed. His pecker had turned red as copper, but it stood straight up. I put my hand on it, and he moved pleasurably at the touch.

My fatigue began to let up a bit. My finger wandered up and down his pecker. The camera started up again.

I sat astraddle him, and it felt good to have him back inside me. My flower closed around him, and I lay down on him, without moving, just with that hard, glistening shaft inside me. It was a good rest position, and I laid my head on his shoulder. Inside me I could feel a faint, pleasant throb.

Safe and satisfied after the violent exertion, I was contracting faintly in my flower. My feelings grew stronger, as if shaving my flower had made it different, more sensitive, and I felt a nice, delicate tingling in there. Yes, the skin outside was obviously more sensitive to the touch now, much more unprotected and alert.

Göran brought out a chair with a low, slanted back, soft and padded but without armrests.

"We'll use the chair now," he said to Heini, who started working on the floodlights.

Mikkel went over and sat down with his legs spread out and his organ erect, taking the last drags of his cigarette before he crushed it in an ashtray that Bengt held out for him. I got up and staggered over to him. I turned my back to him and sat down between his brown legs with my knees together. His pecker slipped right into me, tight as I was down there, and it was very pleasant sitting that way. I leaned back and rested while the camera and the floodlights were being arranged.

When everything was ready, I pulled my legs apart. Taken from in front and from a bit below, without even a spot of fuzz on my flower, I must have given them some fine close-ups of his pecker bulging into me. I moved up and down like a child playing "ride a cockhorse," and it started feeling awfully good again. But then I had to climb off and turn around, facing Mikkel, which wasn't too bad either, since he was so nice-looking.

With one leg down on each side of him, I bent over and bit him on the neck. He held his arms tightly around me, crushing my breasts to his chest. We were going full blast again, and I helped things along by putting my feet on the floor and pushing myself up and down. He started writhing under me, and his smile disappeared. His mouth just hung open without any expression, and his grip got tighter around my waist.

"Cut!" said Göran.

We got up reluctantly.

"Lie on your stomach over the back of the chair," he continued, and I did as he said. Mikkel spread me apart in back. First he just stuck it in between my legs, as the one boy had done with the other from in front. That gave me a funny, helpless feeling, maybe because I was hanging over the back of the chair with my hands in the seat and just the tips of my toes on the floor. He reached around my hips and felt me from the front. I was soaking wet again. He pulled my buttocks wide apart and pushed me forward a little, so my feet were dangling in the air. He put the head of his sex slowly but surely into me, and I closed around his shaft. I squeezed my muscles there and noticed that I could take hold of it, grasp it inside of me and hold it tight. Mikkel breathed heavily and put it farther in. I pulled in the muscles in my crotch and heard him sob out loud. He kept moving it inside me, but I could tell that I had the upper hand. It was out of his control now, and he couldn't help pulling it back and forth, back and forth.

I started getting soft and warm around my whole seat. Something was loosening up in me and starting to flow. Mikkel was right with me. I could tell for sure that he was near the end—his pecker was getting bigger and tensing up. With that, I crept quickly forward in the chair and rolled on down to the floor.

Mikkel stood there with a faraway look in his eyes and his mouth open.

"Good girl!" said Göran. "That's the way to do it! We've got to husband our resources. A couple more quick shots, and you won't have to hold on any more."

While they worked with floodlights, camera, and cables, Mikkel and I spent the time standing in the middle of the floor with our arms around each other, our chests pressed close together. His pecker burned between our stomachs. This was tough, and we were both getting hornier all the time. It wouldn't have taken much to make us curl up together in a bundle on the floor without thinking about our work or the money we were getting for it.

Then we started up again.

I stood upright in the middle of the floor, in front of the spotlights, with my feet slightly apart. I touched the tips of my fingers to my toes, keeping my knees straight, then put my feet a little farther apart and rested the palms of my hands on the floor. Mikkel waited a moment, while my head dangled between my arms, then he got the signal to start from behind. He laughed with joy for a moment, then quieted down. Unable to make another sound, he just poked his organ into me until it felt as if I had it in up to my stomach. (Standing that way, I had it darn near there anyway!) He clutched me with all his strength around the hips, bending forward until he was almost hanging over me. I began to tighten up inside with those rhythmic spasms I now knew so well, when all of a sudden we were interrupted again.

"Stand out there on the floor," said Göran, "put your hands on the back of the armchair and put your feet way back and wide apart and let him at you again."

I did what he said, as did Mikkel. Once I was in position, along he came, but this time he was more deliberate and put it in only a little way.

"Good!" said Göran. "Hold still like that, put your head down on her back and take hold of her breasts."

Mikkel did so, and I noticed that he was close to collapsing again. The camera kept turning.

"Faces to the camera," ordered Göran, "and get going! Now you're free to finish up."

A sheet of flame shot through my body, strongest along my back, and as I stared at the camera it started to happen. It came like a waterfall, and Mikkel began groaning. I think I was crying when his load came, and I remember that my knees were knocking and that I lost my grip on the back of the chair. I ended up lying on the floor, with my bottom pressed hard against him. That's the way we finished each other off, and the two of us finally lay stretched out on the floor, side by side, and everything was over.

"Good!" said Göran. "What a fabulous ending!"

When I got up, I noticed it was all my legs could do to hold me. But Mikkel still had a hard-on.

Not until I was standing under the shower washing the make-up off my face and body did my head clear again. I returned to the studio all washed up and fully clothed. Mikkel had already left, and Göran and Bengt were alone in the studio. My knees were made of rubber, but I felt good inside and clear in the head.

Göran had already written out my check, and he gave it to me right away—three thousand Swedish crowns, as agreed. The two of them were very pleasant, and I curtsied as I took the slip of paper.

"You were great," said Göran, and Bengt nodded agreement. Göran gave me a calling card with his name and "Vitaliafilm Inc." on it. The address was in Stockholm.

"Whenever you feel like doing some more, just come back," he went on. "You were unusually good."

I went down the stairs, out the back door, and through the gate. I headed straight to the bank, where Göran was obviously well known, and cashed the check.

I spent most of the money on travelers' checks and then took a taxi home to my quiet, comfortable women's hotel. I even got the same room, lay down and fell asleep immediately.

For two or three hours I slept the sleep of the just, then woke up, took a shower, and went out to get something to eat.

After eating, I went to a bookstore and bought a fine edition of Fröding's religious verse, in two leather-bound volumes, along with a volume of poems by Strindberg. I put them in my bag and took a solitary, peaceful walk through Göteborg. It's a nice town.

Lazy and satisfied inside, I was glad to be alone again, just walking around and breathing fresh air— not to mention having a good supply of money on me.

I went to bed early that night too, and once again I enjoyed my solitude, free to do what I wanted, with no one in bed beside me. I think the last thing I thought was that in spite of everything it was stupid not to have found out how well Mikkel played the violin.

He was a nice boy.

No, now that I think about it, it was Dr. Peterson I thought about last of all, because I lay there for a while and made up my mind to send him a postcard the very next day. I sketched out a brief message about how good the first days of my trip had been and how healthy his former patient had become. As a doctor, I knew he'd be pleased by that.

I was also happy about the beautiful editions of Strindberg and Fröding that I'd been able to afford.

6

The trip from Göteborg to Copenhagen went easily. I rode first with an elderly married couple, and later with a nice old truckdriver. I paid my own way on the boat.

To make a long story short, I made the trip a virgin and I got off the boat at Copenhagen sweet and clean, with my knapsack on my shoulder.

Then I met dear little Lise.

I was sitting in a restaurant having a sandwich, and Lise saw me from a distance and smiled. I smiled back, in the same way. It was a certain kind of smile. She came right over to me.

"Hi!" she said and sat down at my table.

Lise was one of the sweetest things you could imagine. A couple of years older than me, she had very dark blue eyes, dark eyebrows, and a strange, impudent smile. She had a way of licking the corner of her mouth that I'll never forget. Her waist and hips were narrow but her bosom swelled under her plaid shirt. I told her that I was on a hiking tour through the Continent, and she said that I could stay with her while I was in Copenhagen. As soon as I'd finished my sandwich, we went home to her small apartment.

There she kicked off her sandals and produced a bottle of gin, some mineral water, and a few lemon slices. After a couple of drinks, we were able to talk together freely, and I told of my experience in Göte-

borg. She howled with laughter. Lise was studying
to be an architect, and when I saw how she had arranged her apartment—with unusual taste but undoubtedly at great expense—I asked if she had rich
parents. She laughed again.

"No," she said, "they're not rich. I don't even get
my rent money from them. I live off something else.
I mean, there are some other people who pay for
everything here."

"Who are they?" I asked.

"The embassy and NATO," said Lise, smiling.

"Which embassy?"

"American, of course. They pay the best."

"But don't you have to study during the day if
you're going to finish school?"

"I don't work days for the Allies, only nights."

"Good God," I said, "are you a spy?"

She smiled with her mouth closed. Then she licked
the corner of her mouth.

"Shall I show you what I live off?" she said after
a while.

"Yes," I said tensely.

Without a word she raised up her hips and pulled
off her slacks and panties with a single tug. She lay
there on the sofa, her legs slightly apart, naked from
the navel down. She put her hand on her tight, narrow
sex and said, "This is what I live off."

It really steamed me up to see her naked below the
waist, telling me that she made a living just by having
fun with her flower.

"Do they pay well?" I asked.

"The Americans pay like crazy. As long as we have
UN people, UNESCO, NATO, and the embassy in

Copenhagen, no well-built girl need go without. They pay up to several hundred crowns for it. So I do it only when I feel like it. Once in a while I feel like something else."

I smiled at her. "What do you feel like now?"

"I feel like you," she said. "What do you look like with your clothes off?"

"If you take your own shirt off first," I said, "you'll find out soon enough."

She slipped her shirt off and lay on her side, so that both her breasts hung down. They were bigger than Brita's or mine, and I wanted to feel them against my body. So I got up and undressed, while she gave an interested look at everything that came into view. When I was naked, I sat down on the edge of the sofa and looked at her. She was lovely to see, round and firm, thin and well-developed at the same time.

"You've shaved yourself!" she said loudly. "Let me have a good look."

"It was the make-up man who did that for the movies. It wasn't my idea."

I lay back on the bed so she could see the whole thing. She felt me with her fingers.

"You're all smooth," she said. "It's wonderful to look at. What does it feel like?"

"Nice. The skin is more sensitive like this. I think it makes me a little hornier."

She examined me closely, and I moved so that her right breast touched mine.

We lay like that without putting a hand on each other. My drink tasted fine. She spilled cigarette ashes on my stomach. It was nice just lying there, knowing we had something to look forward to and that we had plenty of time. Lise was sweet enough to eat up, and I started things off by taking one of her breasts in my mouth. She reacted immediately to my tongue.

I kept up my investigation of her breasts until both were like flower buds all ready to burst, warm, red, and hard. I kissed her on the mouth and eyes, licked her in the ears, kissed the back of her neck, bit her in the armpits, and finally turned her over on her stomach. She had a lovely back, and I gave her a long, wet kiss on the small of it. She reacted. I went farther down, noticing that I was wet between the legs myself. My mouth stopped at the spot where the rear end divides in two, and Lise squirmed violently. She couldn't manage to hold that pretty white bottom of hers still, and she was pressing her pelvis hard against the sofa. I pulled her buttocks apart and licked down into the crevice between them. She was warm and damp there, and when I pulled her buttocks farther apart, I could see the pink opening, so tight and little that one would hardly think there was room in it for a matchstick. I stuck my mouth in and kissed it, licked it with the point of my tongue, while she lifted her backside up to receive it.

"Stop," she cried out. "You mustn't! I'm just as sensitive there as in front. Don't do it any more!"

But she stayed in the same position and didn't try to get up. I was the one who stopped. I turned her over on her back and kissed her navel. It was little and tight, about the same as she was in back, except the skin here was white.

My mouth slipped down, and I sucked hard at the

spot where her belly joined the inside of her thigh. I licked her around her whole flower, and when I went to work right at the little, warm, damp spot between the two openings, she groaned slowly and deeply. I did it again and again, without touching the narrow slit itself, which was getting wetter and wetter from inside. Then she got up and looked at me with shiny, dazed eyes.

"Stop right there!" she said in a thick voice. "That was almost too much. Let's go into the bathroom."

She walked ahead of me, took a shower hose down from a hook, and adjusted it to a lukewarm temperature at a fairly high pressure. I climbed into the tub after her. Lise smiled with satisfaction.

I gasped when I felt the powerful spray from the shower against my breasts. First one, then the other. My rosebuds swelled up immediately, red and stiff. She sprayed between my breasts and on the small of my back. Then she quit for a minute.

I yelped when the stream hit me in the crotch. She turned the shower on full blast, and my whole flower began to glow and melt. She let the shower move itself back and forth, while I raised my knees to allow it to get at me better. I had to clutch the sides of the tub. Before long things started moving inside me, and that well-known sensation of everything running in my middle came on full force. But just as the first spasms started, Lise turned the shower off, and I sat back with my hair tousled and my face red.

I had practically lost my voice, but whispered, "Shall I give you a shower?"

"No," she said, "I'm the hostess here. Stand up, please."

She rubbed me dry, and smeared me with salve in front and in back, as if I were a baby.

"Go lie down on the sofa," she said when she was finished, "and I'll be along with something I think will be new for you. But you musn't be afraid . . . promise?"

I wasn't afraid of anything, and I went in and lay down on the sofa, my whole body on fire. I counted the seconds until she got back. Finally she came in, holding something in her hand, something long and stiff with straps attached to it.

"Have you seen one of these before?" she asked and licked the corner of her mouth.

"No," I said. "What on earth—"

Then I saw what it was, and a shock of fright and pleasure went through me. It was a male organ, made of some kind of hard rubber. It was an accurate replica, of medium size, but with somewhat sharper edges and outline. Even the little hole in front was included.

Lise pointed to the rim around the head. "It's better than a real one, you see? And it never gets soft. It can *always* perform."

She placed it against her mount and fastened it with the straps. It was quick work, and soon was firmly attached to her. She took some vaseline on her fingers and rubbed it on the machine.

"Lie on your back," she said. "That's best."

I lay down flat and pulled my knees up, stretching them out to the side. I was in a complete fog and thought she was taking terribly long about it.

Finally she lay down on top of me with the thing

between my legs and her lovely breasts against mine. Then she carefully put it into me.

Just a bit at first.

I gasped, it was such a funny feeling, familiar and new at the same time. She raised her hips and began screwing me, evenly and steadily.

In a way, it *was* better than usual.

The pecker that was boring into me was sharper in shape than a real one, and a little rough at the edges. Lise knew from her own experience how a girl would like it—fast and slow, deep in, all the way out, sudden surprises, then in and out for a while with perfect regularity. But there was more to it than that. Apart from having the feeling of being pierced by a perfect man, I had her soft white skin and her lovely breasts against mine. Her hair hung down in my face, and I was close to passing out. Two or three times that enormous wave came along and carried me off to eternity and away from everything dull, trivial, and tedious. In the course of the evening, we changed places several times. I'm sure Lise enjoyed it as much as I did.

We had nice rest periods too, eating something in her kitchen, drinking and smoking, and talking about our other interests. It turned out that Lise collected old glass, and already had a fine little collection from several countries.

Since I myself was a book collector, she promised to take me along to a well-known secondhand book-dealer the next morning.

We fell asleep in the nude, with our arms around each other's neck.

Both of us were tired and happy.

7

We woke up well rested the next morning. We bathed and got dressed without touching each other, except for an exchange of kisses on the cheek.

At breakfast I said, "Lise, that thing we used last night, is it Danish?"

"Oh no," she said, "I got it from an English girl. They're almost impossible to get in this country. It's a valuable thing, a rarity that you'd never see except in the crime museum. They have a fine collection there."

I said no more and went on eating. She had served delicious rolls and black coffee.

"How was it yesterday?" continued Lise. "Did you like it?"

"Yes," I murmured, "it was fine, but—but I missed something. I don't know what it was."

"Tonight we're having a guest," said Lise cheerfully. "I'm inviting a third to the party."

"A third?" I asked curiously. "Do you mean a boy?"

"Yes," she answered, "a real boy. A nice boy for the two of us."

It ought to be Mikkel, I thought, who can wear out three women. Mikkel, who still had a hard-on right to the end, even after we'd been on the floor.

"Is he any good?" I asked.

"Do you think I'd ask him if he weren't?"

That was a plausible argument. I didn't think Lise

would have invited a third if he wasn't good at it.

She took me to the bookstore and then went about her own business—bright, well-rested, and elegantly dressed.

At the bookstore I found a splendid edition of Kierkegaard and some charming old volumes of Hans Christian Andersen. I put them in my bag and wandered around, looking at the city of Copenhagen, at the Round Tower and the old buildings. I ate a bit of lunch and then went home to Lise's apartment. I had my own key.

I was dusty and warm after my trip around town, so I took a bath—all by myself with the shower hose. It's not a bad invention.

At about seven, Lise came home with Jan.

She fixed us a huge, delicious dinner, complete with wine, and we spent almost two hours at the table. I was looking at Jan the whole time. I forgot to say that first of all we had a drink, actually three of them. Then Lise took her clothes off, and we followed suit. In other words, we were naked the whole time at the table.

Jan was a boy of Lise's age, medium height, quite delicate-looking, and he struck me right off as something of a disappointment if one thought of him as a partner for both of us for the whole evening. But with nothing on he was awfully well built, not so much muscular as firm and well rounded in his body. Not much hair on him—his chest was bare, and only under his arms and below his navel was there some medium-blond hair growing. His plant was of medium size and just a bit bent when it stood up. On the whole, an attractive, sweet boy. He had an unusually friendly, almost bashful way about him, and he was most polite and gallant toward us both. He was an aristocrat, either a baron or a count, I don't remember which.

It was nice to get undressed right away, and we felt free and unembarrassed, like brothers and sisters. Jan was in charge of the wine, and he opened the bottles to air them. As he stood bent over a stubborn cork, Lise walked past him, reached under his legs from behind and took hold of his testicles. He started a bit, but turned around to her and smiled. She hung right on to him, this time from in front, and I could see from his smile what good friends they were. She held his pecker by the tip, and it grew stiff and big right in her fingers.

"Look at it!" she said to me. "Isn't it nice?"

"Oh no," said Jan, "there's nothing unusual about it."

I could see that it was nice, and for a while the three of us stood there together naked, Lise and I each holding on to it with one hand.

Jan cleared his throat. "Excuse me, but I'm opening a bottle."

"Have you noticed that she's shaved?" Lise said to him. "Isn't it nice?"

"She's covering it up," answered Jan. "But in any event it does give one the advantage of getting a better idea of the contours of the human form. I like the idea myself. I believe my family used to do it in the seventeenth century, men and women both. But I've got to air the wine now."

It was a delicious meal, but I was getting hungrier and hungrier for both Jan and Lise. I had something to look forward to, and I enjoyed the waiting time to the hilt. Later I came to understand the secret of Jan's charm; it was a completely relaxed sort of calm that gave the feeling that his friendliness came from within, from something deep inside him. There was absolutely nothing restless or impatient about him. He had himself completely under control. He poured wine carefully into our glasses and took care of everything while we ate.

In the middle of dinner Lise said, "Can't the two of you shave me too? I'd really love it."

"Of course!" said Jan, raising his glass to her. "We'll fix you up fine."

We did too. After dessert.

Dear little Lise had to lie down on her back on the sofa while I got soapy water and a brush and Jan found the shaving set that he used to keep in the apartment. He put in a new blade. Lise lay there smoking and smiling. Every once in a while she licked the corner of her mouth.

When I'd worked the soapy water into suds, Jan and I sat down on the edge of the sofa with Lise between us, so that she had her knees out and her feet on the floor. The food and wine had put us in a good mood, so we talked and laughed as the important project progressed.

I took a handful of suds and put it in the middle of Lise's hair, then spread it slowly around. She stayed on her back, smiling with satisfaction. I rubbed the suds in between her legs and in her pubic hair and once in a while she'd forget to smile, but would shudder involuntarily instead. Jan sat next to her and watched.

After a while he said, "That's enough. They're soft down to the roots now."

I stopped work and scooped the suds off her, just as Bengt had done with me a few days before. Now her bush was wet and curly, but no longer white with soap. I removed the last of the soap with a towel.

Jan began using the scissors on her, cutting her almost bare around the slit, before he used the razor. (Bengt had used an old-fashioned blade.) With just a few strokes, he shaved the hair off at the roots, carefully and in all directions, until not a strand was left. On her bottom, there was nothing at all. Jan and I looked closely. I washed her off in front with lukewarm water and a face cloth, and then we rubbed her thoroughly with cream, making her skin soft and smooth. I sneaked a rub down between her buttocks too, right down to her little pink opening. Lise looked as if she wanted to turn over on her stomach when I did that—just to see the treatment through.

There she lay, smooth and sweet like a thirteen- or fourteen-year-old, but not quite the same shape. It had a unique effect on Jan and me. I put my hand over her slit to feel the dampness coming out of her. She was warm and slick. So was I.

And there was Jan, sitting alone beside two shaved girls.

He remained considerate, polite, and calm through the whole business. And when I lay down on top of Lise, he sat quietly beside us smoking a Turkish cigarette, stroking us in turn between the legs. We were just lying there quietly with our breasts touching each other, and Jan enjoyed watching it. I rubbed my abdomen against hers, and it was lovely to feel that neither of us had hair there. It really was a new feeling. Both Lise and I were damp in the crotch, and Jan's pretty, long pecker had a couple of shiny pearls on the end.

Lise got up. "Let's do something with him," she said with a smile.

We pulled him down between us on the sofa and lay with our breasts against his chest. He still had his cigarette in his mouth. I reached for his organ and met Lise's hand in the same place. The two of us kept a hand around it, while I put my head on his breast and started licking a nipple, which began to swell up just like a girl's. Lise took his cigarette away and put it out. Then she put her arm around his head and kissed him. I went searching farther down with my mouth, and soon I was licking up the fine, shiny drops on the end of his pecker. I licked him all over down there—on the testicles, underneath them, at the root of his plant, and on its underside. Then I put the end of it in my mouth. But I was careful—I didn't want any seed spilled ahead of schedule. He lay completely still and didn't make a sound. Then Lise's head came down to mine, and the two of us licked him together.

All at once Lise raised her head and turned to me, "We'll draw lots for who goes first."

Jan fetched two matchsticks from the table. He broke one of them in two. Then he held them out to us.

"The longer one goes first," he said.

We drew. Lise got the whole match.

"Don't be unhappy," she said to me. "It's great fun watching too."

"The one who watches gets to decide the positions," said I. "That's the least she can ask for."

They agreed.

"Lie down on your back on the table," I said to Lise, and we quickly got rid of everything that was in the way. She lay down on her back and raised her legs up in the air, so that her seat was right at the edge of the table. Jan went over to her and she put her legs on his shoulders. It was a good position, which showed plainly everything Lise had to offer. You could see her whole, smooth, hairless flower and her firm little buttocks. Jan put his pecker up to her slit, which seemed to open by itself. He pushed it in a bit, and Lise gave out a long, heart-rending sigh. Her hands banged on the surface of the table when Jan pulled it out of her again. I could see everything perfectly, but only from above—the stiff, bluish organ slipping easily into the slit, the contractions in her muscles each time it happened. But I wanted to see more.

After a period of experimentation, I found a position for them that I liked best to watch.

Jan lay back on the sofa with his feet on the floor. Lise sat astride him, found her opening, and put his organ at the entrance to it. She let herself down on his pecker. Then she lay down on him with her breasts and stomach against his. From behind, I had a magnificent view of the whole thing. He kept his legs together and she kept hers apart, and his pecker stood up from his testicles like a tall candle, right into her crotch, either all or part way. Because she had her legs apart, I could see everything that was hidden between her openings. It was marvelous to see how Jan's big thick shaft slipped so easily into that wet slit that looked so tiny—and how Lise shut herself around the shaft again, almost sucking it in like some kind of animal. Everything was in view at the same time; her anus and the little space in front of it, her open flower dripping honey, his organ sticking into it, and his testicles hanging down in their soft, warm sac. By now they were quite occupied with their work; Lise was breathing heavily, and Jan was writhing and groaning underneath her.

I kept watching and just couldn't keep my hands off those working organs. I touched his pecker and got a finger all the way around it, then let the fingers of both hands fondle his sac and her openings. It was touchy work with her shaved. I slid my fingers up along the bottom of the crevice formed by her spread legs, stopped at the opening in her rear, and put in my stiff, slippery finger. She shrieked with joy. I kept it in there a while, holding his testicles with my other hand, fingering them gently. Then I stuck my head in among the four legs and bit him on his pecker, which was hard as a rock. I kept at it with my mouth, both in her slit and on his testicles—or else sometimes just licking at his pecker. Gradually the two of them got farther and farther away from the world around them. With my finger inside Lise I could tell that the spasms were beginning, and I felt violent contractions in the root of his pecker. They knotted themselves in a tangle of arms and legs, jamming their groins together, and rolled around the sofa. Jan bared his teeth and shut his eyes, while Lise screamed with her mouth wide open. It was good to see them come at the same time. They were such good friends, and each was thinking as much of the other as of himself.

They lay exhausted and sweaty beside each other on the sofa. I gave them each a cigarette and got two glasses of white wine from the refrigerator. They lay quietly in each other's arms, just enjoying it all, and of course I was happy to see it, but thought that things didn't look too good for me. His plant hung long and soft between his legs. I joined them, with a glass of my own in my hand.

Lise smiled. "You're next, Lillian," she murmured.

I took his organ in my hand and pressed it between my fingers.

"It doesn't look that way," I said. They both laughed.

When we'd finished the wine, I got up. "Let's go in the bathroom and try the shower hose on Jan."

"Good!" said Lise, and we took him by both hands and pulled him up from the sofa. In the bathroom we put him in the tub and I adjusted the shower to warm water and high pressure. Jan shuddered when the blast hit his testicles, and after I'd showered his pecker for a while it raised its head again. I washed it in lukewarm soapy water, rinsed the suds off, and gave his organ a good rubdown with suntan lotion. He was in splendid form now and wanted to go back to the sofa.

Lise lay down first, propped up with pillows in a sitting position, with her back to the wall. She pulled

me down on her so that I had my head against her
breast and my legs out front. She held me under the
arms with a hand on each of my breasts.

"You lie this way," she said, and I raised my knees
up and spread them out so that Jan could get in. He
entered between my legs in the usual way and got to
work. By now it was high time, as I was in a real
state from watching the two of them. Jan did a fine,
gentle job, quite deliberate about it and thinking more
of me than of himself. Jan was a real prince. I was
also enjoying Lise's attentions—she was rubbing my
breasts and kissing me on the mouth and face. When
I cut loose, it was like an avalanche carrying us all
away; we curled up in a big clump, and I could feel
the tears running down my cheeks.

We took a break now, had something to eat and
talked about glass, books, and our various experiences.

Finally Lise said, "Now it's Jan's turn. He's been
giving out all along, and now he should be taken care
of. He likes best of all to be worked on while
he watches girls loving each other."

"You're a dear," said Jan in his friendly way, "but
don't go to any trouble for my sake. I've been doing
fine all along."

We had Jan sit down on the sofa and we lay down
together in front of him. We did everything girls can
do with each other, and Jan just sat back and watched,
relaxed and satisfied, his flagpole standing at atten-
tion. He was obviously enjoying it. So were we.

Lise went and got her machine. Jan gave a broad
smile. "Good for you!" he said. "Good for you!"

Now we went at it in front of him in every position

we could think of—frontward, backward, from underneath, and from on top. Jan sat there watching, smoking and smiling. While I was down on all fours and
Lise was working on me from behind, I managed to
crawl over to Jan and take his pecker in my mouth.
It was about time, for he was more steamed up now
than ever, and he soon started jerking his legs. When
the gush came, I took the whole thing in my mouth
and for the first time tasted the marvelous, bitter
flavor of sperm. I threw myself over on my back, and
Lise finished me off from in front.

That night the three of us slept on Lise's sofa,
which opened into a bed.

Next morning we started in again, almost before
we woke up, still warm and relaxed from sleep. Jan
lay on his back, and we sat on top of him, I straddling his hips and Lise kneeling with her flower against
his mouth. This way, Lise and I could kiss each other
and massage each other's breasts. We struggled
around on the daybed until we were finished. Then for
coffee, eggs, and rolls with marmalade. We were all
hungry and in good spirits.

I spent the morning alone at the Glyptotek, looking
at their Egyptian collection, and afterward went back
to my bookdealer. But I didn't find anything I was
especially interested in.

That afternoon I said good-bye to Lise; we both
cried a little at the thought of parting. I hit the road
once again, my knapsack on my back and a fair-
sized bundle of books lashed to it.

By evening I'd crossed the border to Germany. I
stopped at an old inn in a little country town with
slanted roofs and storks on the eaves. I had a lovely,

solitary sleep on a deep, soft German bed, with quilts both over and under me.

I don't remember falling asleep, because I was so tired and full of new impressions from my travels.

8

Cocoa with hardboiled eggs and anchovies make up my favorite breakfast. That's what I was eating next morning at the inn where I'd spent my first night in northern Germany. I'd had a look at my travel funds, which were in fine shape from the unexpected money I'd earned in Sweden and from having been Lise's guest for my entire stay in Denmark. After meeting Jan, a count, and Lise, daughter of a railroad worker, I couldn't have thought more highly of Danish hospitality.

I was nevertheless brooding: Jan's dad had been (or still was) a count, and Lise's dad was a railroad watchman. My own father was a businessman of the middle class—or maybe a little above it, but not much. And yet we'd had fun together without any noticeable disturbances due to the class struggle. (Of course, I know perfectly well that Scandinavia doesn't have class distinctions. I learned it in school and I've read it in the papers. It's required reading for all registered voters, but it's still not true.) There was no doubt that it was the god Sexus who had united us, and we had him, and him alone, to thank for the fact that this young count and the middle-class girl, together with a daughter of the common people, had gotten along naturally and without prejudice the way we had.

I drank some more cocoa and ate another egg.

Before me lay Germany.

First stop: Hamburg.

I had plenty of informative literature with me. I knew which museums and theaters I wanted to see, and I'd made up my mind to rent a rowboat at the Hotel Atlantic and go rowing on the Alster. I'd also included a visit to St. Paul's and the Reeperbahn, the famous amusement section that's so eagerly sought out by Scandinavian visitors. Especially by men in their fifties.

I stayed for twenty-four hours—no, a little more, for two nights—at this inn of mine, caught up on my sleep, paid a modest bill, and resolved to lead a proper, vigorous life in the days ahead.

Ach!

Something happened in Hamburg that scared me out of my wits. And it began on the Reeperbahn. I had reached town in the afternoon after getting rides with two truck drivers. I walked along the Alster, watching the sailboats, then went window shopping. Hamburg is a clean, very rich town. It must have at least seven million shiny new cars, and the slums were bombed out in times past and were replaced by attractive developments once Germany, Russia, and the United States had won the war against Poland, England, and the Jews.

That evening I walked up along the Reeperbahn, taking in the gaudy lights, the placards and restaurant entrances. A row of small movie houses advertised "broad-minded" shows. Although I'd played in this kind of film, I'd never seen one, and I was tense when I sat down in the dark. A little later I began to laugh. Not because the movie was funny, but because it didn't show anything more than two people,

half-dressed at first and then naked, swimming in a
brook in the forest and then sunning themselves on a
blanket. It was absolutely proper, and when I com-
pared it with the film we'd made in Göteborg, I could
hardly help laughing. After half an hour of this I
walked out and strolled among the strange streets of
the Reeperbahn. Everything was lighted up, shiny
and very "sinful" to look at, but in some way it was
artificial. I went into a cabaret that advertised naked
dancing; it was pathetic—neither dancing nor any
immodesty at all. I soon walked out.

The whole Reeperbahn is dominated by a big police
station, which looms like a tower over the long, wide
street. It serves as a guardian of morals and seems to
do the job very thoroughly.

I stopped at a bookstore that had books with naked
women on the covers. Leafing through them, I found
nothing that was amusing, exciting, or new. I thought
they must be some kind of children's books, and I
wondered how people could serve up such thin gruel. I
ended up buying an old edition of Hölderlin's
Hyperion and two volumes of Heine's poems. They
were cheap, and feeling pleased with the transaction,
I thought of finding a hotel and going to bed.

But I'd made up my mind to see sinful Hamburg
by night, so I gritted my teeth and picked out a new
restaurant.

Inside, the place was thick with smoke and had a
dance floor and orchestra platform. I ordered a glass
of Moselle wine and sat down to look around. Everything seemed quite normal.

Then in came the orchestra.

First a giant of a woman in a sort of weird national

costume, I suppose from some forsaken Alpine valley. Then five enormous men, each as fat as the other and all of them in children's shirts and kneepants with straps over their shoulders. The huge stomachs were crammed in behind music stands and the fat, hairy knees bent so that the kneepants split at the seams. The lady giant took a position as conductor, and from the audience came not a roar but an explosion, a peal of thunder. The building seemed to tremble under the salvos of clapping and howling. I found myself gasping for air, and something inside me—my heart, I think —stopped for an instant. The peal of thunder from the audience was actually a greeting to the orchestra.

People stamped their feet and beat the palms of their hands on the tables, sending huge beer mugs hopping into the air.

The Alpine queen turned her enormous form toward the audience and raised up her arms, causing her breasts to fill her blond-colored blouse to the bursting point. The cheering mounted a few degrees, and I felt myself getting really scared. Some couples flung themselves onto the dance floor, while the rest kept on howling.

At this point a shriek cut through the air, hard and sharp as an air-raid siren. It was one of the man-mountains in the orchestra who had stood up next to the woman to acknowledge the greeting. He howled with all his strength, and the rest of the orchestra joined in with him.

I felt like Stanley in darkest Africa, hunting for a Dr. Livingstone who had not survived—a dead, slaughtered, murdered, spitted, roasted, and eaten Dr. Livingstone. I was inconceivably alone with the savages—savages who perhaps were not evil in themselves, but who were going to devour me anyway, simply because that was the custom—a tradition they'd inherited from their ancestors.

Suddenly a new element was added to the ear-splitting din. This time it was war drums, at superhuman volume. The orchestra intoned the first few beats, and then the entire hall screamed along with it. It must have been a melody which everyone there knew but which no foreign ear could grasp. The hall was still filling up, and several people had sat at my table and were howling along, while their feet pounded the floor and their hands banged on the table, on the chairs and on their hefty thighs. I was surrounded on all sides, and the way to the exit seemed to stretch out forever. I knew I could never reach it, and I felt so awfully tiny. All I could think of was getting out of this cannibal village before they ate me up.

This was just the beginning. It got steadily worse.

The orchestra was really going by now, and the whole hall surged and rocked with the din. People grasped each other by the hands or the arms and roared. How could I leave the restaurant and get out of this country alive? Did I still have a chance, just half a chance, of getting away?

More and more of the giants were dancing, hollering, sweating, embracing. The orchestra did their work as if they were wielding clubs and sledge hammers, and as time went by the whole thing did come to have a rhythm to it, or anyway a sort of beat—people were little by little doing and screaming the same things together. The members of the orchestra gasped for breath, lifted up their superstomachs and groaned to the rhythm; they raised their wide, fat knees and pounded the floor with dreadful force. Like enraged hippopotamuses, like rhinoceroses in heat, they beat on the oaken floors. They were pouring with sweat, and a few of them were having a fight in a corner. Someone was up on a table, bellowing. Blood was flowing. And the sound blended into an uncanny, rhythmic, stupendous roar that repeated itself over and over again. These were the countrymen of Novalis, von Platen, and Rilke dancing and giving expression to their joy and vitality. The music and the roaring now took the form of a short, rocking melody—the same thing time and again. Then came the scariest part. The most horrible moment of all was upon me. Hölderlin's race had found itself at last, and they all sang together, with the orchestra, time after time, in a beat like a huge army on the march, shouting the words for half an hour, for an eternity, over and over again, the same two lines:

Wein, Wein, Wein!
Wurst, Wurst, Wurst!
Wein, Wein, Wein!
Wurst, Wurst, Wurst!

That was when I fled, forcing my way with all my strength past backsides and stomachs, between beer barrels and chair backs, under double chins, and behind huge shoulders with bulging red necks above them. I forged ahead, reached the door, the cloakroom, and then caught sight of the outer door far away. I mustered my strength, tipped the doorman, but the noise in the restaurant was as strong as ever, a series

of bombs exploding, with a constant crashing din and
a horrifying, massive chorus:

Wein, Wein, Wein!
Wurst, Wurst, Wurst!

They kept on and on. It had already lasted an
eternity, but time had stopped. They kept on with
their music and their song celebration. They kept on.
I heard them from out on the sidewalk:

Wein, Wein, Wein!
Wurst, Wurst, Wurst!

They kept it up. They never stopped. I believe—
no, I *know* they never stopped. It's the great, eternal
Teutonic tom-tom. It will never end. It will ring out
over all Europe.

I stood out on the street in the mild summer evening,
wet with tears of terror, certain they would have
eaten me alive, or at least boiled me down to soap,
if I hadn't escaped by some miracle.

Some hero or other must have rescued me.

Out on the sidewalk, I looked again at the entrance
door. When you came right down to it, it was a
perfectly proper place, with an orchestra from Bavaria
—some place or other in Bavaria, Allgäu or the
Lord knows where—and the restaurant announced
that it was *"preiswert"* and had excellent sausages.
It was a spot where one could have fun in a natural,
socially acceptable way and take the children along—
in short, a family place, a splendid, substantial es-
tablishment for good folk. And when I thought about
it, I remembered that I actually had seen children in

that howling, tramping, roaring, hump-backed bomb burst of a family hell.

Obviously it's not a certainty they would have boiled me down to actual soap—maybe they'd only have made children's soap out of my youthful fat.

Who knows?

Maybe all German children's soap is boiled from Scandinavian girls of my age. Maybe there's really no white-slave traffic after all—the girls who've disappeared through the years have actually ended up at a German soap factory, soft and mild for the delicate skins of German children.

This visit to a family restaurant on the Reeperbahn didn't discourage me. A few blocks away I found a cellar spot that looked much more attractive. I went in and found a small table under some red Japanese lanterns. Out in the middle, instead of the usual dance floor, there was something that looked like a pool. It had no water in it, but something else—dark and unclear.

It *was* clear that I'd arrived just in time.

I had hardly ordered a drink before the performance began. Two huge, muscular, fat, and almost naked women in their fifties came in. Raising their hands over their heads, they waved, touching off an enthusiastic, expectant howl from the audience. Both women wore bras over their enormous breasts—not the usual thing made out of cloth, but something hard and firm, some kind of stiff rubber and canvas, or something like that. They were wearing tight bikini pants to cover their crotches. Totally paralyzed, I couldn't help but stare. Both had short haircuts. People rose from their tables, and some tried to find places closer up.

The two women climbed down into the strange pool. They separated, one in each corner, and I could see their bare feet sinking down in mud. That was what the pool contained. They stared at each other, then a spectator whistled. A couple of others roared out insults. The giantesses stalked toward each other with threatening grimaces, arms hanging at their sides. When they had gotten quite close to each other, the audience howled again, and a few people whistled out of contempt for the poor fighting spirit the two were showing.

All at once one of them grabbed the other by the wrist and twisted it around. The other shrieked with pain, bent backward, and kicked her opponent in the stomach. The first one lost her wristhold and doubled up in agony. While she was standing that way, the other grabbed her by the hair with both hands and tugged at it until she fell over. She had enough life left in her to grab her opponent's leg on the way down. Now the two of them thrashed about in the mud, pulling each other's hair, trying to break each other's fingers, and so forth. They rolled around in the slime, first the one on top and then the other. After a few seconds, you couldn't tell them apart, and hair, arms, bodies, and legs were just shades of black and gray. The audience was beside itself, and obviously knew both of them by their first names, since they called out "Irma" and "Pauline". I found it absolutely impossible to see the slightest difference between the two bundles of muscles; both were covered with mud from head to toe, and the only human-looking thing about them was the whites of their eyes, which occasionally flashed through the mud. You could see they had gotten slippery from the mud and had trouble holding onto each other. Breaking a finger, spraining an ankle, or twisting an arm over the other's back was almost an impossibility.

Most of the spectators were on their feet.

They roared incessantly, and had begun throwing things—beer steins, napkins, empty bottles—at the combatants. Everyone was enjoying himself to the hilt. And when the two grunting wrestlers finally managed to get to their feet and to start fighting all over again, I thought the cheering would lift the roof off the place. The two Amazons threw themselves at each other's hair, broke apart, kicked at each other, and tried to get wrestling holds. They threw mud in each other's face, aiming for the eyes, and both kept shrieking, half from pain and half to intimidate the other.

The fervor of Mozart's compatriots in the audience mounted steadily. The two combatants tumbled down again, one landing astride the other's back and trying to press her face into the mud. The victim shrieked and gurgled like a maniac. This was the high point so far, and it unleased a new shower of glasses and beer bottles, all aimed at the head of the one underneath.

I was paralyzed, just scared stiff. I would have wet my pants if it had been possible—I mean if I hadn't just been to the toilet out in the hall.

The two heroines struggled on, but the one on the bottom succeeded in twisting herself free. She got

hold of the other's foot and twisted it, while her opponent cut loose with a piercing scream. Now it was
her turn to lie face down in the mud, and she got
back everything she had given the other before.

I don't remember anything else except that I was
standing by the door trying to get out. A policeman
was holding me back, a big, broad-shouldered man
from the "morality police," *Sittlichkeitspolizei*. A
screaming waitress stood next to me and held me, until
finally I realized that it all had to do with paying my
check. I came up with the money and was turned
loose into the dark outside. I set off down the block
in order to calm myself and get some fresh air. It
struck me that the mud battle exhibition must be
under the supervision of the morality police and thus
have the law's blessing. It was good to know that
Hamburg's city fathers kept an eye on sports this way,
making sure that nothing improper, indecent, or un-
clean went on before the eyes of an unprotected
audience.

I turned up a side street, and all at once noticed
that I was in a crowd. Between two houses stood
a sort of entryway consisting of huge iron gates, not
shut but arranged in much the same way as the entrance to a public urinal. However, everything was
much larger. It was obvious that some sort of street
or square lay inside the iron gates. But what was it?

It looked like the entrance to a prison or a jail,
and I was dying to find out what lay behind those
iron gates. A bit nervous, I walked in and right away
realized what I had come into. It was a street about
a hundred yards long, on both sides of which were
large store windows. Next to each window was a door,

just like on a street of little shops—places for selling meat, fish, and game. And that's just what they were —show windows for butcher shops. But you should have seen what kind of meat was on sale. In the windows sat half-naked girls and women of all ages and in all kinds of outlandish get-ups, from young things to sixty-year-olds, some of them with just their bottoms bare, some in corsets, some with bare breasts, some with high-button shoes on, and a couple with riding crops. The whole thing was the most unreal sight I'd ever seen, and I had to look around me. I was the only female on the street. All the rest were men or young boys going from window to window and looking at the display of white, medium, and dark meat on display there. It all reminded me of something I'd seen pictures of, maybe movies too. This red-light street was a combination comfort station and concentration camp. I looked around for a moment, then noticed that someone was beginning to howl here too. Someone was laughing at the same time, but the howling kept getting louder, whereupon it dawned on me that it was the girls behind the windows who were doing the howling and that it was me they were howling at. A couple of them opened their windows and shrieked at me. I won't repeat what they said, but it wasn't nice. My head spun, and I started running down the street in wild flight with windows and howling women on either side of me, as I did my best to zig-zag between drunk, laughing men standing in groups or sauntering along individually. At the far end of the street there was the same kind of iron gate as at the entrance, and I dashed out at full speed, so frightened that I ran across the street and over to a newsstand. I only knew that no matter what it cost, I had to get away from this armor-plated, virtuous, police-inspected German family paradise, although I realized that in reality I was not in danger. But it wasn't reality I was afraid of; it was something quite different. Something hidden.

In front of me stood a gentleman with newspapers under his arm. I say "gentleman" because that's exactly what he was. His car, a black Mercedes, was parked in front of the newsstand, so you could tell he'd just gotten out to buy some papers. I stopped in front of him, panting for breath, my hair dangling over my eyes. He looked friendly and reassuring. There was something homey about him, and also something quite correct, almost rigid, even about his posture.

"May I be of any assistance?" he said with great politeness.

"Yes," I said, "can you give me a ride away from here?"

He opened the door graciously and I got in and sat down. He walked around the car and took his place behind the wheel.

He drove up the Reeperbahn and into the city. We hardly said a word to each other, but he gave me a cigarette, which I lit and puffed at.

He sat there in silence, as if in deep thought, and when I took a look at him he struck me as a cultured but melancholy person.

All at once he said, "Is there some particular place you'd like to be dropped off? Do you have a hotel for the night?"

"No," I said. "I haven't checked in any place yet." He didn't seem surprised.

"Then I'll drive you to a good place. I don't think it's quite right for you to wander around on your own this way."

"Thank you very much," I said. And I meant every word of it.

He drove away from the busy city streets into the outskirts of town. He remained silent and kept his melancholy expression.

"I know an excellent little hotel, almost a sort of rooming house," was all he said.

Then suddenly he added, "Have you had supper?"

"No," I said. I'd had a couple of drinks in the course of the evening, but they hadn't affected me. I realized that I was hungry.

"Then we'll drive some place and eat together," he said. "I mean, of course, if you don't mind?"

I looked at him from the side. He was about fifty years old and good-looking. Correct and cultured. And always that strange, quiet, sad expression. He was certainly not fat, but quite powerfully built—and extremely well dressed, without looking ridiculously over-elegant like a lot of prosperous Germans. In other words, he wasn't making an effort to dress in such a way that everyone would be sure to notice that he had plenty of money.

"No," I said, dragging out my answer as I felt that mysterious feminine need to seem hard-to-get, however dishonest, deceitful, or untruthful such an appearance might be. Of course I wanted to go out and eat with him—he looked nice, had money, and had been behaving in a way that made me feel calm and safe. And I didn't doubt that he knew which restaurants were the ones to go to in Hamburg. What's more, he was sure to pick up the check, and that would help my travel budget. Nevertheless I yielded to the need to pretend that I didn't really feel like it. Untruthfulness is deep-rooted in human beings. And this was exactly what Dr. Peterson had worked so hard to break in me—pretending I didn't like what I really did like. He'd even taught me to say it right out—I like this and that—without feeling ashamed of myself.

"I'd love to go out and eat with you," I said frankly.

He turned back and drove toward the center of town.

"I could even ask you to eat at home with me this evening," he said after a while, "but my wife and children are away at a small place we have on the Mediterranean, so I'm home alone—aside from the butler, who's at home—but maybe it wouldn't be altogether proper. You're so young . . . I really don't know how it would look."

"You're very correct about things," I said. I now began to get really interested in him—a house on the Mediterranean, a butler at home . . . well. Count Jan had undoubtedly had a butler at home, but for me it was something new.

"Ah, perhaps I'm too correct," he said softly, "but that's the way I was brought up. I was originally trained as an army officer and spent several years with the general staff, although I was quite young. Later I managed one of the big steel factories here and then a bank. Of course I realize how wrong it is of me to invite a young lady to eat at my house, but I assure you that no offense is intended. I beg you not to think ill of me."

"I'd love to eat supper at your house," I said. It could be fun to be waited on by a real servant. He stopped the car and made a phone call from a booth by the road.

"You must excuse me," he said when he came back, "but I was just giving the butler orders to set the table and have a meal ready for you."

We drove on through town, over to the other side —I don't really know where—and finally drove through a large gateway into the grounds of a huge mansion. There was a chauffeur's cottage at the entrance and several other buildings on the grounds.

The table was set when we arrived. The servant, who certainly didn't look like an aristocratic English butler but who was round and fat, poured drinks for us and retired. My host was a Mozart enthusiast, and we talked about music as we ate.

I stood in his luxurious bedroom and pulled my panties off while he stood there, completely dressed, looking at me. I got rid of my shirt and bra in a hurry, too, while he just looked—with the same melancholy expression he'd had earlier in the evening. In his hand he had a long rubber strap, which he'd doubled up to make it shorter and thicker. I knew I was alone with him in that big house, and I was scared to death. I was so frightened I could feel the sweat running ice-cold from my armpits along my sides.

His mouth was half open, and he was breathing hard as he stared at me.

With the rubber strap in one hand, he came over to me and let his other hand slide over my breasts a couple of times. He was short of breath and smiling, but his face looked distressed all the same. The only thing I could think of was to do whatever he wanted —just to get away unharmed.

At length he took off his trousers and underpants. His mighty pecker was standing straight out, heavy, stiff, and wet. In the midst of everything, I felt like touching it, but I was much too frightened to do anything. I was filled with a weird combination of terror and desire. He took off his shirt and stood beside me naked.

"You don't have to be afraid," he said gently. "It doesn't really hurt so much—no more than you can stand anyway, and this strap can't possibly harm you. Nothing will be broken. But don't scream too loudly, and try not to make things difficult. That's all there is to it."

He pointed at the floor. "Lie down," he said.

I got down on all fours with my bottom up.

Immediately I felt a blow from the rubber strap, quick and hard—it struck me in the groove between the buttocks. It was worse than I had expected, and stung like salt in a wound. With a howl, I threw myself over on my back with my hands over my behind. In the same instant, the strap whistled through the air a second time, and struck me in front, across the bottom part of my stomach. Maybe it wasn't quite so hard this time, but it hurt like the devil, and while I heard myself howl, he hit me again, this time across the front of my thighs. That made me turn over on my stomach again and pull my legs up underneath me. I felt tears running down my cheeks. Right away, he hit me again from behind, and I think this blow was harder than the first; it cut me across the seat and burned like fire. I turned around and held my hands behind to protect myself, and instantly he hit me two or three more times in front, on the stomach, across the thighs, and higher up. I rolled screaming around the floor, sprang up, and ran behind a chair.

He came after me with the strap in his right hand. I was holding my hands down, one in front and one in back. Quickly and mercilessly he struck me across the breast, and the second I bent over forward I got the strap with full force across my back.

He stopped and looked at me. His organ was stiff and red, bulging out like an enormous flower, and in spite of the pain I was feeling I wanted to touch it, lick at it, take it in my mouth, feel it between my legs or my breasts—and get it into me.

He still looked sad, and his voice sounded polite when he talked to me again. He spoke apologetically.

"You must forgive me," he said, "but this is the only pleasure I have. The only kind I can have. In a while I'm finished. And I'll try not to hit too hard. Lie down on the bed, please."

I lay face down, and all at once I noticed I wasn't afraid any more. I raised my backside up a little. He went on hitting me, not so hard now, but repeatedly. I stopped crying, and gradually I felt as if the pain from the beating was dividing into two parts: it hurt, and at the same time something inside me was starting to flow. My crotch itched, and I turned over on my back and spread my knees apart. He understood and beat me on the inside of my thighs, on my abdomen, and even on my flower. I pulled my knees right up to my ears, and once again he gave me hard, whistling blows in back until I turned over on my stomach again. He beat me across the backside and down across my legs, up across my whole back and shoulders. Then came some more violent blows across the seat, so hard that I started screaming again and held my hands over my bottom.

Then he stopped.

His voice was husky, and he had difficulty speaking as he handed me the rubber strap.

"Hit me," he said softly. "Now it's my turn. Please. You won't regret it."

I was hot and sweaty, and my whole body was covered with red streaks. In my crotch and between my buttocks I was wet and squishy.

He lay down on his back.

Then he took my left hand and pulled it down to his big, warm, shiny pecker with the round sack underneath.

"Hold on hard," he said, "and hit me at the same time. Hold on as hard as you can!"

I grabbed his organ and squeezed it with all the strength I had while I hit him hard with the strap on his stomach, legs, and chest. He writhed under the blows and my hold on him, then suddenly lifted up his knees and held his hands over his face. At the same time the spasms began coming, and the warm fluid poured out of him in three or four long spurts over my hands and arm.

He lay quiet for a while, then took his hands from his face and sat up on the edge of the bed. I don't think I've ever seen a human being look so wretched.

I woke up next morning in a quiet, attractive hotel room. The first thing I noticed was that my back was sore. I got up and examined myself in the mirror. Only my backside carried traces of last night's adventures; it had stripes like a zebra's. Undoubtedly it was the very first and hardest blows that had left marks. I was so sore back there that it hurt to sit down without a cushion under me.

I went to the telephone and ordered breakfast: grapefruit juice, cocoa, eggs and anchovies. Also a large glass of milk. I showered, dried myself, and took it easy.

I found almost a thousand extra German marks in my purse.

Still, I'd had enough of Hamburg, and the only thing I wanted to see before traveling on was the Hagenbeck zoo.

I slung my knapsack on my back and took the streetcar to the zoo. As I wandered about there, memories of the Reeperbahn and my millionaire's mansion ran through my head. I walked from cage to cage, from the antelopes to the apes and the tigers, and I began feeling a little more at ease; it was like being among humans again.

9

The next day I was standing by the exit of a gas station along the autobahn. A few cars drove by without picking me up. Then I met Freddy. He had stopped for gasoline and was driving a small, old-fashioned, rather cute English sports car—the kind which still looks like a car and which I like much better than the newer type, which looks more like a sausage.

Freddy was an Englishman, I suppose about forty. He had graying blond hair and was wearing an old sweater and worn yellow pigskin gloves. I jumped in beside him, and it was fun to switch to English after talking so much German. I am fond of foreign languages and have no trouble speaking German and English fluently. Freddy was on his way to Italy, which is where I wanted to go too. We drove together through Germany and Switzerland, calmly and peacefully, often taking narrower roads to avoid the worst of the traffic. It was great traveling through the Alps that way.

It was all the more peaceful since Freddy didn't so much as hold my hand. Once in a while he'd look at me, but he never touched me. We drove together for four or five days and spent every night in a hotel or rooming house, but in separate rooms and without his even giving me a good-night kiss on the cheek.

Freddy drank.

Not so that he got drunk or even muddle-headed.

The only thing noticeable was that now and then he'd speak more slowly and deliberately than otherwise. That meant he'd had a few. But he was never visibly affected. Yet he drank from morning to night. He had his first glass before breakfast, and his second barely an hour afterward. When he was driving, he always had a flask in the glove compartment, and my job was to fill his glass or light his cigarette for him. He never spoke of himself, never confided in me, and never said a coarse or improper word. When we had driven down the south side of the Alps and come into Italy, it appeared that he knew all there was to know about cities, churches, museums, works of art, and architecture. He talked a lot about them, and we took our time driving from town to town, all over Tuscany.

Freddy was an art historian, and the only thing I ever learned about his past was that he'd been raised in boarding schools and had served in the Royal Air Force during the war. His constant drinking had no effect at all on his driving. He drove calmly, steadily, and correctly all the time.

When a bottle was empty, we just threw it out of the car and got a new one from the supply under his seat. In Italy he drank nothing but Grappa, which I never particularly cared for myself.

One night the inevitable happened—the hotel had only one vacant room left.

"O.K.," said Freddy, "I'll sleep on the couch." The room did have a sofa in addition to a double bed.

After my stay in Hamburg I still had streaks on

my behind, though they were no longer very tender. And while we sauntered around town that evening, going from bar to bar, I wondered what was going to happen when we went up to our room together. Freddy, never sober and never drunk, would undoubtedly play it cool as usual, and I made up my mind to show him my black-and-blue spots and to tell him what had happened to me in Germany. I figured he would just shake his head and say, "Bloody Germans." But I wanted to soften him up a little beforehand, so in one of the bars I said, "Do you like me, Freddy?"

"Of course," he answered in a serious but friendly way. "I like you very much. A whole lot."

"Haven't you ever thought of kissing me on the cheek?" I said.

"I certainly have," he said, "I've thought of it often, but—"

"But what?"

"I've thought of a lot of other things too."

He said nothing further, and we walked around some more and then home to the hotel. In the room he immediately opened up a new bottle and poured himself half a tumbler while I got undressed. I noticed him watching me with interest and approval. With my bra still on, but my behind bare, I walked over to him and bent over so that he could see my marks. He took a look at them and felt my buttocks gently as I told him about my bank president in Teutonia.

"Hmm," he said and shook his head. "Bloody Germans!"

I lay face down across his knees so that he could see my wounds more closely. Then I took off my bra and sat up on his lap.

"Freddy," I said, "is there anything wrong with me?"

"No," he said.

"Don't you want to go to bed with me?" I asked. And believe me, I really wanted to.

"Yes, I do," said Freddy, "I really do. But *you* wouldn't get any fun out of it."

"Are you sure?" I said.

"Yes, I am."

"Why?"

"Because I can't satisfy you," he said.

"You can't?" I asked. I let my hand slip down to his fly and felt around. I found out that he could too—there was no doubt about it; it was long and hard. I undid his zipper.

"Not the way you'd want me to," he answered.

"It doesn't matter what I want," I said softly. "The important thing is for you to enjoy it. Go ahead and do anything you want."

He undressed, put the bottle and glass on the night table, and we lay down. He was calm, relaxed and nice, and we lay close together, kissing each other. I licked his nipples, which he liked, and he did the same to me. I could feel his pecker pressed hard and nice against me.

He put it between my legs, as if I were a boy, and it felt lovely there. It had gotten wet and slippery, partly from itself and partly from all the smooth honey that was collecting at my slit. But he didn't touch me there. He turned me over on my stomach and got up on top of me, with his pecker still between my legs. He lay there for a long time without making a move, and I got awfully upset about his being so still while I was waiting so long. He just lay on my back almost motionless, with his mouth against the back of my neck or between my shoulder blades. All of a sudden he got up on his knees.

"Raise up a little," he said and took me around the hips.

I lifted my behind up toward him and rested on all fours.

"Fine," he said.

For a second I felt his shaft up between my legs, where he rubbed the end of it against my flower, just a tiny bit inside me, to make himself good and slippery. Then he pulled apart my buttocks, and I knew that that tight little opening of mine in the back was visible in all its beauty.

He put his slick pecker up against the tiny opening and then slowly, little by little, pushed it into my rear end. It was a shock, but it didn't really hurt so much. He put it in up to the hilt, and I could feel his testicles against my flower. It was a feeling difficult to describe, but the strange thing is that it was uncannily like the other opening in one way, and at the same time so different, if only because the feeling went in a different direction—back in and up to my hips and the small of my back, even up along my spine. I writhed and squirmed, because it felt so good and hurt at the same time. I noticed that I was flowing inside in the usual way, and when I shut my eyes I couldn't tell for sure which opening he was working on. The whole business just rolled up together inside me, both in my abdomen and in back. My muscles had begun to tense in rhythm and now I couldn't keep still. I let my head hang down between my arms, with my eyes shut and my mouth open, and the waves started coming over me in earnest. Unable to stay on all fours any longer, I lay down on my stomach, and he came right along, still inside my tight opening with his huge plant, pulling it in and out, in and out. I felt his full weight on me, and I pressed my backside up against him. Then I started squirming, and only half-consciously I felt myself coming, like a waterfall, and the same unbelievable feeling went through my abdomen and my back.

I screamed out loud while this was going on, and when I was almost finished I felt him coming too. I got his whole load up my insides just like an enema.

From that day on we always shared a room wherever we spent the night, and every single day we did it in the same way, always from behind, between my buttocks, in the tight, narrow opening in back.

After a week I was just as sore back there as I had been when I left Germany, but in a less mentionable way.

After ten days I had to ask Freddy to stop. He did, but he wouldn't—or couldn't—do it any other way.

We had gradually traveled a long way south and were getting close to Naples. Being sore behind, I always used a cushion on the rather hard seat of his car. But in any event I got over the soreness faster this time than before. I think this was because I rubbed myself thoroughly in back with oil and salve, and once in a while I wished Freddy would try it again.

It did happen again in Naples, and in a way I'll never forget.

One afternoon, when I came home to our hotel room, Freddy was there, but not alone. He had with him a boy of about fifteen, and the boy was stark naked. They obviously knew each other from before, and it confirmed the fact that this was not Freddy's first time in Naples.

The boy was brown and well-built, almost girlish, and he had no hair on his body except for a tiny little tuft around his plant. I felt a yearning for him right away and started taking off my clothes. It was just as clear what Freddy wanted, and he started getting undressed too. The boy's tool stood straight up the minute I took off the first garment, and he lay down on the bed face up, smiling with chalk-white teeth. I leaned down and kissed him on the mouth and then over his whole body. His fine, straight tool was as big as a grown man's, and I licked it all over, bit at it, and put it in my mouth, while Freddy sat on the edge of the bed and smoked a cigarette. The boy twisted and squirmed. I got on top of him and rubbed my breasts against his body, until his eyes were damp and all he could do was groan and writhe. Freddy arranged the boy on the edge of the bed with his legs out, and I sat down on him, very carefully, and got his pecker in the right opening. As I slid down on him I felt him pushing into me in front. I moved carefully up and down, and noticed that Freddy was fooling around between our legs. Then all at once something unexpected happened. With the boy inside me in front, Freddy pulled my buttocks apart and put his own tool into the opening in back, deep in. I collapsed completely and fell forward, my head on the boy's shoulder, my behind up in the air. I hardly remember what happened, but the three of us kept at it with each other several times. I had the feeling that I kept coming for half an hour.

Afterward I slept until Freddy and I went out and had supper together—the boy had left while I was sleeping.

That evening I realized that I wanted to be alone again, and two days later I was sitting in a third-class car on the way to Paris—by myself.

I was heading back north.

10

Paris.

No, there's nothing left to tell. Or rather, nothing that concerns anyone but me. My private life. In Paris, I met Pierre, and I . . . well, I sort of . . . yes, I'm embarrassed to say . . . I fell in love.

Pierre is a mechanic and a metal worker.

His French is a little difficult to understand. But the minute I saw him an electric shock went through me. I watched him working. I watched him straightening out an automobile rim with a vise and a long hammer as his only tools, cold, measuring with his eye, exactly as if he were working with the most delicate instruments. It was while I watched his hands, so thin and strong and so precise in everything they did, that I understood what art was and what it takes to paint a great picture—generations and generations of people like Pierre, craftsmen of his type.

He looked up and smiled, and I asked if he knew of a reasonable hotel in the neighborhood, although I already had one. He walked with me to a small hotel a few blocks away and got me a room. Then he went back to his shop, and that evening we had dinner together at an inexpensive restaurant. At the end, he smiled at me over his wine glass.

"Faire l'amour?" he said softly.

"Oui!" I said.

We started kissing each other out on the street, and we kept it up in bed. I stayed in his arms for a long time, and we were lying face to face. Afterward, still face to face, in the same way, with me on my back. He did it superbly—slowly, gently, and deeply, always in the same way.

He never varied anything. He was perfect, just as he was when he was hammering out that rim the first time I saw him. Whatever Pierre did was perfect.

And when something's perfect, there's no way to tell about it.

11

It's autumn.

And I'm through writing.

My trip is over; I've had my turn out in the wide world. I've left home, and I have a place of my own. Outside the window, the trees are yellow and orange. Some of the leaves are red. I have around me the books I bought on my trip, as well as those I had before and some new ones for my studies. I am calm, content, and clear-headed—I enjoy reading and working.

In Ecclesiastes it says that everything has its time: there's a time for sowing, a time for reaping. "There is a time to break down and a time to build up."

For me the time is come when the air is clear and cool. It's fall, the season that's spring for the soul. It's my time of year.

This completed book that lies before me contains not one obscene word; it's just a description of things that have happened, and I can tell about them in my own speech, without all the "earthy" words whose tastelessness and ugliness show nothing except that those who use them hate and despise what they're talking about. Readers who miss these words from the underworld of the middle class still have a chance: I'm going to suggest that a few blank pages be left in the book, where the reader can write in all the words he misses; but if that's not possible, then he or she can write them in the margin. Never, when

I've slept with someone or lived with someone, have I felt the need for these "forbidden" words. I'm sorry, but to me they have a sound which I don't like and which seems untrue because they give a false picture of things as they are.

I met a man on this trip, a human being. This was Pierre. He is just about the only "normal," healthy man I've ever met.

I feel like recalling Dr. Peterson's words about there not being any special "sexual morality," but just the same human morality as in all other things. Man's sexual pleasures are nothing to have a guilty conscience about, because it's not one's own conscience, but an inherited one, mother's, grandmother's or greatgrandmother's conscience. I don't mean that one shouldn't have a conscience. One certainly should— but one should have one's own conscience.

Pierre was a man who could be a lover without being ashamed of it, but without being proud of it either. And he was a good worker, an artist and a craftsman.

But without Dr. Peterson, and without the things I had experienced beforehand, I would never have understood Pierre, I could never have appreciated him.

But the trip is over, and it's fall, with cold and clearness in the air. There's a time to sow and a time to reap.

I feel calm, and I'm going to work this winter. But one thing occurs to me—that people agree without further ado that a young man should (in fact, *must*) be given time to learn to know the world, "gather experience," "have his fling," or whatever you may call it. For him to "gain experience" with women assumes that he has a partner, that two persons (or at least two) are involved. But what about his partner? How firmly we all believe it: what's permissible for a young man—what in fact is considered an advantage, having "worldly experience"—is for his counterpart of the opposite sex anything but an advantage, in fact, a stain, a disgrace that marks her for life, something that can never be washed away.

And the firmest of all in that attitude are the traveling family men on business trips to the brothels of Hamburg and Paris. They're the ones who are disturbed over the world's immorality.

That's why I've written down a few things as accurately as I could; I've tried to write the truth— without a stitch.

On the wall hangs my diaphragm in a light-blue silk ribbon . . .